Yet another party-girl approached him, and yet again he dismissed her—to her displeasure. He flicked his eyes back to the dancers, but as he did so there was a sudden gap in his eyeline to the far side of the room.

Everything stopped. Every faculty stopped. Except one.

Vision.

And one other. Memory

Burning, coruscating, vi

Like a zombie, he started to walk forward. His face was a mask, his pulse insensible.

Into the vortex.

Towards the one human being he had *never* wanted to see again for the rest of his life. But who was standing there, across the room, staring at him with an expression of absolute shock on her face. For a moment it was like a knife slicing open his guts.

Emotion lashed through him, whipping up from deep inside—from a place he had long, long since buried. Reanimating him.

Shock was still uppermost in him, but he was controlling it now. Channelling it. Focussing it. Targeting it.

Targeting it on the one person he had wanted never again to see in this world. His sole lapse of judgement. His one mistake.

Sophie Granton.

Julia James lives in England with her family. Mills & Boon® were the first 'grown-up' books she read as a teenager, alongside Georgette Heyer and Daphne du Maurier, and she's been reading them ever since. Julia adores the English and Celtic countryside, in all its seasons, and is fascinated by all things historical, from castles to cottages. She also has a special love for the Mediterranean—'The most perfect landscape after England'!—and considers both ideal settings for romance stories. In between writing she enjoys walking, gardening, needlework, baking extremely gooey cakes and trying to stay fit!

PENNILESS
AND PURCHASED

BY
JULIA JAMES

MILLS & BOON

First published in Great Britain 2010
Harlequin Mills & Boon Limited,
Eton House, 18-24 Paradise Road, Richmond, Surrey TW9 1SR

© Julia James 2010

ISBN: 978 0 263 87796 0

Harlequin Mills & Boon policy is to use papers that are natural, renewable and recyclable products and made from wood grown in sustainable forests. The logging and manufacturing process conform to the legal environmental regulations of the country of origin.

Printed and bound in Spain
by Litografia Rosés, S.A., Barcelona

PENNILESS
AND PURCHASED

CHAPTER ONE

SOPHIE stood, holding herself motionless, quite still. She stared, unblinking, at the reflection staring back at her in the long mirror of the hotel's powder room. The woman in the mirror looked out at her with the same expressionless stare.

She was wearing a clinging, low-cut satin evening dress, her blond hair slicked with hairspray around one shoulder. Her eyes were heavy with glittery make-up, lashes loaded down with coal-black mascara, skin larded with foundation, earlobes dripping crystal, mouth sticky with scarlet lipstick.

It isn't me!

The cry came from somewhere very deep in Sophie. Very deep. Like a buried place. A grave.

The grave of the person she once had been.

Would never be again.

Heaviness lay like a deadweight in her stomach, wound around by revulsion at what she could see in the mirror.

'Excuse me—'

The voice was clipped, impatient, wanting Sophie to move aside. Jerkily, she did so, catching the look of unveiled contempt in the older woman's eyes as she took her place to inspect her appearance. Sophie knew what she had seen. Knew why the woman had looked contemptuous. She felt her stomach churn again. The inside of her mouth was dry, and she poured herself a glass of water from the jug placed on the vanity unit for the use of guests, gulping it down as if it could still her turmoil. For one final time, she stared at herself bleakly in the mirror. Then, with a sudden short intake of breath that cut like glass in her throat, she seized up her evening bag and walked out of the powder room with a stiff, taut gait, on heels so high they swayed her body despite the rigidity in her aching leg muscles as she forced herself to keep going.

Across the hotel lobby, in the bar, her client was waiting for her.

Nikos Kazandros glanced around him. The vast, opulently decorated reception room was dimly lit, crowded, and noisy with thumping music and too-loud voices. It was exactly the kind of party Nikos avoided—full of louche, hedonistic people in search of kicks that inevitably involved entertainment that ran to little white lines and the indiscriminate use of bedrooms. A frown formed on Nikos's darkly planed face.

His reluctance to go in was not echoed by his companion.

'Nik—c'mon. This party's going to be really hot!'

Georgias's voice was slurred. Since his father was a long-time friend of Nikos's own father, Nikos had taken on the role of minder to the impressionable twenty-two-year-old for the younger man's brief stopover in London. For Nikos, a show and dinner would have been enough, but Georgias had wanted to party. Knowing that if he acted too heavy-handed the kid would cut and run and end up God knew where, Nikos had temporised. He would give Georgias an hour here max, no more, and make sure the only stimulant he imbibed was alcohol.

Not that drugs would be the only temptation here. The

place was heaving with girls, the kind who—Nikos's lip curled in contempt—flocked wherever wealthy men partied, eager to make themselves accessible to them. He and Georgias had already been sized up, and a moment later a blonde with more hair than dress was inviting them to dance. Nikos let Georgias take up the invitation with alacrity, turning down with a curt shake of his head the immediate follow-on invite from a brunette who had also scented fresh meat. She flounced off with a pout, leaving Nikos propping the wall up, a cynical twist to his mouth, counting the minutes till he could call time on Georgias and get the hell out of here.

Girls like those here held no attraction for him. Barely one step away from hookers, they made it clear their sole interest in a man was the size of his wallet. They traded sex for a lush lifestyle.

Their one virtue was that they were perfectly open about it.

For a moment Nikos's face closed fast. Some lacked even that virtue…concealing to the last their real interest…

Some could look as innocent as the morning dew, and all the time—

No. Automatically, as it had done repeatedly for four years now, the guillotine sliced down.

He'd made a mistake. Been a fool. Worse than a fool. But he'd pulled back in time—just in time. For a microsecond, nothing more, bleakness filled his eyes. Then it was gone, replaced by a hardness that etched the features of his face, set his high cheekbones into relief below his dark, long-lashed eyes.

Yet another party-girl approached him, and yet again he dismissed her, to her displeasure. His eyes flicked back to the dancers, to keep Georgias in his view. But as he did so, there was a sudden gap in his eyeline to the far side of the room.

Everything stopped. Every faculty he possessed stopped working. Except one.

Vision.

And one other. Memory.

Burning, coruscating, vicious memory.

Like a zombie, he started to walk forward. His face was a mask, his pulse insensible.

Into the vortex.

Towards the one human being he had *never* wanted to see again for the rest of his life, but who was standing there, across the room, staring at him with an expression of absolute shock on her face. For a moment it was like a knife slicing open his guts. His eyes flicked to the man beside her.

What the hell—? Nikos recognised him, but not with pleasure. Cosmo Dimistris was a man well at home at parties like this. And well at home with the kind of women who frequented them. Nikos's eyes lasered back to the woman at Cosmo's side, her closeness telling him exactly what she was doing there.

Cosmo's wealth telling him exactly why she was there.

So she was still playing the same game...still hanging out with rich men.

Emotion lashed through him, whipping up from deep inside—from a place he had long, long since buried. Shock was still uppermost in him, but he was controlling it now. Channelling it. Focussing it. Targeting it.

Targeting it on the one person who had been his sole lapse of judgement. His one mistake.

Sophie Granton.

Sophie felt her face beneath the mask of her make-up freeze. No, she thought faintly through the numb miasma in her head, it couldn't be! It just couldn't! Not him—not here—not now.

But it was him. Nikos Kazandros. The name tolled in her brain. Tolling her fate. Her doom.

Her eyes could not tear themselves from him. Could not move from the hard, sculpted planes of his face, the sable hair, slashing cheekbones and the night-dark eyes. Could not move from the lean, packed muscle of his six-foot height, the lithe length of his leg, the panthered grace of his stride.

Nikos Kazandros—walking out of the past. Making her oblivious to everything—everything except him. Oblivious to the man she was with, whose company had been anathema to her all evening.

She had made it through drinks at the hotel bar, followed by dinner, over which he had regaled her with boasting about his wealth and possessions, while she had smiled fixedly and asked flattering questions as if she cared less. Then they had arrived at this nightmare party that they seemed to have been at for hours. A sick headache was pressing around her temples, and her stomach was still churning at what she was doing, and why. Sophie had tried desperately to cling to the numbness, just to see her through the remainder of this hideous evening.

And now that numbness had been blasted away as if by nuclear detonation, in one hideous, appalling moment. The moment of ghastly recognition of the man walking towards her.

Nikos Kazandros.

Somewhere, wildly, like a trapped, panicking bird, she could feel thoughts battering around inside her skull. How could it be him? How *could* it? At a place like this?

It hadn't taken her more than thirty shocked seconds to stare around at the lavish penthouse apartment, with the pounding music and the alcohol and drugs circulating freely, and the men cut from the same cloth as the one at her side, and the women—the women looking just the way she did…

To see Nikos Kazandros here, at a party like this…

Memory stabbed through her head.

Covent Garden, a gala night, the men in black tie, the women glittering in jewellery and designer gowns, with the world's greatest tenor and soprano pouring out their voices on stage. Nikos in evening dress, immaculate, devastating, and herself, sitting beside him in their dress circle seats, so quiveringly, shiveringly aware of him…

Nikos glancing towards her, with eyes that held in them an expression that made her heart turn over…

The guillotine sliced down. The one that had been slicing down through her brain for four long, endless, punishing years. Cutting out Nikos Kazandros.

As he made his way towards her, Nikos could take in the full impact of her appearance. Kohled eyes, slicked hair, scarlet mouth, trashy dress. Revulsion curled in him. So this was Sophie Granton now. Four years on. In a place like this. For a brief, knifing moment he felt a different revulsion.

That she should have come to this!

Memory skidded through his head, but he banished it. She had never existed, the girl he'd thought her to be. She'd been someone he'd made up, created for himself out of his own delusions. Delusions that had come crashing down when Sophie Granton had shown what she really wanted.

His mouth twisted. *Not me. Just the Kazandros money. To save the family coffers.*

He came up to her, stood looking down at her. The look of shock had gone from her face, wiped as if he'd never seen in it. Now her face was blank. Empty. There was no sign that she thought there was anything incongruous about her presence here. Or her appearance. Or who she was with and why. For a second, he just let his hard gaze flick over her. Then it was gone. He glanced at the man at her side, acknowledging his recognition of him.

'Cosmo—'

'Nik—'

There was a moment's pause, then the other man said, his voice at once both oleaginous and mocking, speaking in their native language, 'Well, well, this is a new departure for you, Nik. Finally decided to lighten up? Are you with anyone, or are you just going to help yourself to what's on offer? I must say some of the girls here look even more tempting than the one I've brought along. If you're on your own you can take your pick of them.'

His eyes went greedily out over the room, where the assembled female flesh for hire was displaying itself, but his hand had closed possessively over Sophie's wrist all the same, Nikos saw. Stamping his ownership. Again, Nikos felt the thrust of revulsion ice through him.

As Cosmo's hot, stubby fingers closed around her, Sophie swallowed. She'd been trying to avoid the slightest physical contact all evening, but now, with horror opening like a pit beneath her feet, as Nikos Kazandros walked out of the nightmare past into the nightmare present, she was almost grateful for it. Grateful, too, that she could not understand what was being said between the two men.

When she'd realised that the man she was to meet that evening had a Greek name, she'd felt as if the gods themselves were mocking her. Bitterness had risen in her throat, as well as revulsion, and revulsion had twisted through her again when she had walked up to him in the hotel bar some three hours earlier. Greek he might be, but Cosmo Dimistris was as physically different from the only Greek man she knew as a warthog from a leopard. Shorter than her in her high heels, overweight, face like putty, with hot, lascivious eyes, and hands with stumpy fingers and damp palms.

Well, she thought viciously, what did she expect? If a man had to pay for a woman's company in the evening he would hardly be an Adonis, would he? Against her will, her eyes went to the man standing opposite now, and the contrast with the man at her side was cruel and stark. Oh, dear God, he hadn't changed! Not in four agonisingly long years! He was still the most devastating man she had ever laid eyes on! Even now, with a look of killing contempt in his night-dark eyes, she could feel his power as his gaze razored over her. She knew what he saw, even though she had masked her own expression with a blankness that cost her all her strength to hold in place. For a terrible moment, she felt his contempt like a physical blow, shaming and searing her. Then the lasering glance was gone, and he was looking back at Cosmo Dimistris.

'I'm minding Georgias Panotis—Anatole Panotis's son,' he said tersely. 'The kid's wet behind the ears.' He nodded to where Georgias was still close, dancing with the girl with more hair than dress.

Cosmo gave a coarse laugh. 'Going to spoil his fun?'

'Like the fun you have?' His voice was edged, and once more his eyes went to the woman who was going to provide Cosmo Dimistris's 'fun' tonight.

Nikos felt emotion cresting through him like a dark, killing anger. Out of nowhere, like a black tide, he felt the urge to wrest Cosmo's hand from her wrist, tell him to go and find his fun somewhere else! He clamped it down, quelling it by force, slamming down the lid on it as if it were glowing nuclear waste. Sophie Granton was not worth a microgram of emotion—not a moment more of his time. Not then, not now.

His eyes flicked over her one last time. She showed nothing in her eyes now. Nothing after the first shock of recognition. Or was it dismay? He felt the question sting. Yes, he thought with turbid anger, why not dismay? Four years ago she had nearly, so very nearly, succeeded in making a fool of him. Well, she would deceive no one now! He could look at her with impunity. With the only kind of look she deserved. His mouth twisted in contempt as his eyes flicked over her again. She was blanking him, he could see, and his eyes narrowed. There was something about her blankness, her closed, expressionless face, that sent a stab of anger through him. She hadn't been like that when he'd peeled her off him.

Tears, sobbing, clinging to him, clutching at him.

Cosmo was speaking again, and Nikos made himself listen. 'Speaking of fun…I need some of the powder kind.' He dropped Sophie's wrist and changed to English. 'Stay right there, baby.'

To Sophie's dismay, he headed off across the room, to be promptly pounced on by a trio of girls, none of whose attention seemed to bother him. She stared after him. Where was he going? Why? Panic broke through. Dear God, she couldn't be left here like this—with Nikos Kazandros right in front of her. She made to lurch forward, but it was too late. A single word stayed her.

'Sophie.'

Behind the frozen mask of her face, as if a searing flame had scorched the ice in her mind, dissolving the chains and padlocks, the bars and bolts she had put around the past, like a dam being breached, memory came drowning in. Unbearable, agonising memory.

The past, pouring through her head like molten lead….

CHAPTER TWO

THE spring sun was warm on her head, even in the early evening, as Sophie walked through Holland Park, up from Kensington High Street, where she'd hopped off the bus. She loved taking this walk, especially at this time of year. Was there ever a time of year more lovely? she thought. Bars of Schumann's 'Spring Symphony' trilled euphonically through her head as she walked lightly through the park, where trees were unfurling their greenery, the air sweet, even for London.

She quickened her pace. She wanted to tell her father the wonderful news, that she'd been chosen as one of the soloists for the college concert next month. Her mind ran through the repertoire. The two Chopin nocturnes were easy enough, but the Liszt was fiendish! Well, practice would make perfect. It was a shame they weren't going to get the new baby grand that her father had promised her for her birthday earlier in the year, but the existing one was perfectly good enough, and she mustn't be greedy.

She frowned very slightly. It was unlike her father to stint on anything to do with her music. He'd been her biggest enthusiast, from the moment her primary school music teacher had said she really should have piano lessons. From then on her father had paid willingly for anything and everything that developing her talent, such as it was, required. Oh, she was no musical genius. She knew that, accepted that. So very few musicians were, and, considering how incredibly hard it was even for the exceptionally gifted to make a living, she didn't envy them. No, she was perfectly content being talented, dedicated—and amateur. Besides, she made rueful the acknowledgement that she was in the highly privileged position of not having to earn a living. Even when she left college she could continue with her music without any thought of having to make it pay in any way. She would play for pleasure—and other people's, too, she hoped.

Certainly her father loved to listen to her. Again, a rueful smile tugged at her lips. He might be her biggest fan, but his ear was not musical.

'Oh, Daddy, that's Handel, not Bach!'

She heard herself laugh affectionately in her memory.

'Whatever you say, Sophie, pet, whatever you say,' Edward Granton would reply indulgently.

Yes, *indulgence* was definitely the word when it came to her, his daughter, Sophie knew. But although she knew she was the apple of his eye she had never taken advantage of it other than to pursue her music. Besides…a tiny glint of sadness shadowed in her eyes…she knew why her father wanted to indulge her so.

She was all he had.

Her memories of her mother were dim, almost non-existent. She could remember her singing, that was all, a low, clear voice, lulling her to sleep as an infant.

'That's where you get your music from,' her father would tell her, over and over again. *'Your wonderful, wonderful mother.'* Then he would sigh, and Sophie's heart would squeeze with terrible sadness.

So she let him spoil her, for he loved to do so, and she could not deprive him of what gave him so much pleasure. She tried very hard not to *be* spoilt, though she knew that compared with many of the other students, she was. Her father could pay the music college fees without blinking, never burdening her with student loans or the like. She could continue to live at home, in the beautiful house in Holland Park, and have a first-class instrument to practise on, and her clothes were always beautiful because her father liked to see her look pretty.

'You're so like your mother, pet,' he would say. *'She'd be so proud of you. As proud as I am.'*

Well, she wanted her father to be proud of her, wanted to see him smiling at her. Another little frown flickered across her brow. Her father's smiles hadn't been as forthcoming for the past few months, ever since her birthday, really, she supposed. Oh, he wasn't cross or grumpy—it was more that he seemed…preoccupied. As if things were on his mind.

She'd asked him once, when his brow had seemed particularly drawn. But all he'd said to her had been, *'Oh, just the market…the market. Things will pick up again. They always do. They go in cycles.'*

For a while she'd been worried about him. But then she'd had exams coming up, and all her focus had been on them. When she'd surfaced on the other side of the exams it had been the vacation, and she'd had a chance to visit Vienna on a college trip. She'd grabbed it with both hands, and, though her father had blinked a moment when she'd said how much it would cost, he'd handed her a cheque to cover it all the same.

The trip had been every bit as wonderful as she'd known it would be, and so had the extra excursion to Salzberg, which she hadn't been able to resist signing up for, even if had cost a lot. But it had been worth it. She'd brought her father back a huge box of Mozartkugeln to show her appreciation. He'd thanked her with the air of preoccupation that still seemed to be his dominant mood, and listened absently while she'd regaled him with all the wonderful things she'd done and seen. Then he'd headed for his study.

'I've got to make some phone calls, pet,' he'd said, and she hadn't seen him again all evening.

It was unlike him not to want her company, and the following day over breakfast she had taken a deep breath and asked him if things were all right.

'Now, I'm not having you worrying about things that you don't have to worry about,' he'd said firmly. *'Business has its ups and downs, and that's that. Everyone's affected at the moment—it's the recession. That's all.'*

And that was all she had got out of him. But then he never talked business to her. She hardly even knew what exactly Granton plc did. It was property and finance and City things like that, and even though sometimes she felt she ought to be more interested she knew she wasn't, and she also knew her father didn't want her to be. He was a doting parent, but old-fashioned, too. He far preferred her to be off doing something artistic, like music, and the closest she ever got to his business life was when he invited business associates to dinner, and Sophie, as she had done since she was in sixth form, played hostess.

Sophie's mind ran on, pleasantly occupied, until she reached the exit of the park. The roads around here were quiet, and rich with almond blossom, and she caught her breath in delight as she swung homewards along the pavement. She was still gazing upwards into the laden branches as she paused to cross the road to her father's house. There was very little traffic here, and she was about to step into the road, her hand half reaching upwards to cup a cascade of

peach and white blossom, when the throaty throb of a powerful machine prowled down the road. It drew her eye immediately. Low and lean and jet-black, with a world-famous
logo on the elongated bonnet. But it wasn't just the open-
topped car that made her pause. It was the driver.

She felt her lips part. *Wow!* If you wanted an image of Mr
Cool, that was it! Hair as jet-black as his motor, one besuited
arm crooked casually over the lowered driver's window, hands
curving around the steering wheel, white cuffs, a glimpse of
a dark red silk tie, and a face—*oh, gulp*—a face that had a
chiselled profile and—double gulp—dark glasses to die for...

She just stared as he went by. Transfixed.

Too transfixed to see his head shift, very slightly, to bring
her into his line of sight in his rearview mirror, which caught
her perfectly, standing, poised, long pale hair streaming, blue
gypsy skirt wound about her long legs, her hand cupping almond blossoms, petals drifting down over her, caught in a
pool of sunlight.

The car seemed to slow a moment, then picked up speed
again, turning the corner. With a little sigh, Sophie set off in
the same direction. Five minutes later, she was outside their
house, her eyes going to the gleaming back monster parked
a couple of bays along. There was no sign of the driver.

A new neighbour?

She felt her insides give a little skip.

But more likely he was just visiting someone.

A woman, probably. Sophie's imagination fired. She'd be
dark and svelte, with figure-hugging clothes and a sultry
voice. Instinctively she felt her hackles rise. She hated the entirely fictitious female instantly. Then, with a shake of her
head at her own daft imagination, she set her bags down and
set to find her keys.

Letting herself in, she dumped her bags on the chest in the hallway and glanced at her reflection in the mirror above. Long hair, somewhat wispy from the breeze and walking, an oval face, grey-blue eyes, wide set, not much make-up, just a touch of mascara and lip gloss, and little gypsy earrings, which she'd chosen to go with her skirt.

Feeling her hands sticky from London buses, she nipped into the downstairs loo to freshen up. Then she went upstairs. She had the attic floor all to herself. Her father had had it converted to a teenager's dream pad for her thirteenth birthday, and, although it had been redecorated several times since then, she still loved it. Sophie had been going to head straight up to her own rooms, as she knew her father wouldn't be home yet, but as she passed along the first-floor landing she heard her father's voice from the drawing room.

Smilingly, she changed tack, opened the double doors, and sailed in.

'Daddy! How lovely! I didn't know you were home—' she began.

Then she stopped dead. Her father wasn't alone. There was someone else in the large room with him. Sophie heard her breath catch in her throat as her eyes went to the other occupant.

It was the driver of the car that had passed her.

Standing here, he looked even more fantastic than he had in the brief glimpse she'd got of him. He was tall—taller than her and her father. And slim, like a blade, wearing a suit so fantastically cut she knew it screamed Italian designer, just like the pristine white shirt and the dark slash of a tie did, too. But it wasn't his clothes that made the breath catch in her throat, her pulse quicken suddenly. It was the body inside the suit, and the face—oh, the face—that was every bit as chiselled as it had been in profile, with jawline and cheekbones and nose and above all *eyes* that were dark and long-lashed, and which were looking at her and making her feel…feel…

'Sophie, pet, let me introduce you to our guest.'

Her father's voice made her blink, but her gaze was still on the man standing in the middle of the drawing room. Looking—

Drop-dead gorgeous. That was the phrase, and it suited him totally, utterly. Just—drop-dead gorgeous. She wanted to go on staring—couldn't do anything *but* go on staring!

He took her breath away. Literally.

'This is Nikos Kazandros. This is my daughter, Sophie.'

Nikos Kazandros. She echoed the name in her head, and it seemed to resonate like a fine vibration. So he was Greek, she registered. *Nikos Kazandros.* Dreamily, she rolled the name around her head as, dimly, she heard her father perform the introductions. Even more dimly she heard herself murmuring something polite. But then Nikos Kazandros was holding out his hand, saying something to her in a low voice which did not register, only the deep timbre and the slight drawl over the words, the foreign accent hardly there beneath the impeccable English. Numbly, she slipped her hand into his.

His palm and fingers were cool and strong, and as she made contact, she felt another of those strange vibrations go through her. Then she was slipping her hand from his, but continuing to stand there, still gazing at him. Eyes locked to his face.

Long lashes swept down suddenly over his dark eyes, and she felt her breath catch again. Then her father was talking once more.

'My daughter is a student, Mr Kazandros, but I'm fortunate enough that she chooses to live here, not in some student dive.' He gave a brief social laugh.

The dark eyes were on her once more, and she felt their impact with another whoosh in her lungs.

'What do you study?' he asked, addressing her direct.

Again, the deep, slightly accented voice did things to her.

And the eyes, those eyes resting on her, so dark, so very dark…

'Music,' she answered, her voice slightly breathless.

'Indeed? Which instrument do you specialise in?' It was a polite query, nothing more than the circumstances warranted, mere small talk between a guest and the daughter of his host. But there seemed to her to be something deeply profound about the question. Something that made her pulse flutter.

'Piano,' she answered. One-word answers seemed all that she was capable of.

'I'm sure Sophie will play for us after dinner,' said Edward Granton. His daughter's eyes flew to his.

'Is Mr Kazandros staying for dinner?'

'Your father has been so kind as to invite me,' murmured their guest. There was smoothness in his voice now, and the dark lashes were veiling his eyes. 'I hope that does not inconvenience you?'

'Oh, no! No—not at all,' she said, her voice still breathy. Then a smile broke across her face. 'It would be lovely!'

His eyes stilled, rested on her. She saw, deep in those dark, long-lashed orbs, something that once more seemed to hit that strange, evocative frequency that she'd felt when she'd heard his voice. For one long, incredible moment she could not tear her eyes away. She seemed to be falling into their depths, and she could feel her eyes widening, widening…

Her father's voice brought her back. 'Sophie, I've let Mrs T know, but it would be good if you popped in to ask if she needs a hand. Now, very tediously for you, I must speak business to Mr Kazandros, so—'

She took her cue. 'Yes, of course. I'll…um…I'll see you

later.' She nodded briefly, courteously, at the man who was taking her breath away, then turned to go to the door, knowing that what she really wanted to do was go on standing there, gazing at him, drinking him in....

He was before her at the door, opening it for her. Then, as she paused, he smiled down at her suddenly.

'Almond blossom,' he murmured, and his fingers brushed with absolute lightness at a couple of stray petals still caught in her hair. Her eyes flared again, and she felt quivery. Breathless.

'Thank you,' she husked, and suddenly she was too shy to look at him any more.

She all but scurried out of the room. As she gained the landing, she realised her heart was thudding. Forgetting her father's suggestion to go and see the housekeeper, instead Sophie ran upstairs, panting at little by the time she was up in her attic quarters. She threw herself bouncingly down on the bed, feeling her heart give a little thrill.

Nikos Kazandros. His name flared in her brain, and she said it out loud, just to hear the syllables roll around in all their exotic foreignness. What on earth was he doing here? When her father invited business colleagues and associates they were all middle-aged men and dead boring. But this man—oh, wow! He could be a film star, not a businessman.

She gave an exuberant little laugh. She didn't care what he was—he was here, in the house, and in just a little while she'd be seeing him again.

She leapt to her feet, horror-struck. What time was it? She and her father usually dined at eight, so how much time did that leave her? She seized her bedside clock and gave an anguished cry. Could she be ready in time?

Not ready for dinner. Ready for Nikos Kazandros.

Nikos Kazandros, Nikos Kazandros...

The syllables went round and round in her head while she dived into the bathroom and the shower, dragging off her clothes. She had some serious, *serious* ablutions to make!

Nikos was listening to Edward Granton, but his attention was not on what the older man was saying. He knew what it would be about, anyway, and he knew exactly what to expect, and exactly what to do.

But what he had *not* expected was what had happened ten minutes ago in the drawing room.

Thee mou, the girl was a peach! The clearest, most delicately scented honey possible. Even now, with time to compose himself, he could still feel the resonance of the moment the doors had flung open and she'd sailed in. He'd had a moment's vision of flying golden locks, a swirl of colour around her hips and legs, and then every last gram of his focus had gone to her face. He'd recognised it instantly—the girl he'd seen in his rearview mirror, framed like a picture.

An exquisite picture. Stopping him in his tracks.

But she was young. Too young. She didn't look more than eighteen, and Edward Granton had said she was a student. Pity. Pity she was so young. Pity she was his host's daughter. Pity that he was here on business, not pleasure.

Nikos turned his attention back fully on Edward Granton and the figures the older man was presenting, the argument he was making, the proposal he was constructing. Speaking convincingly, persuasively, fluently—and completely failing, all the same, to conceal the fact that he was hovering on the brink of financial ruin. The complete collapse of Granton plc.

Would Kazandros Corp throw Granton the lifeline he was desperate for? Maybe. There was value in the company, no doubt about that, but it was haemorrhaging cash. Granton had made some rash calls, and then had done what so many men under pressure went on to do—made even rasher ones, trying to claw back safety. But safety was gone. Granton was running out of options, running out of room to manoeuvre. Running out, worst of all, of time. In just under a month he'd have to make a hefty payment due on a loan, and right now his cashflow couldn't meet it. After that, things were just going to get worse. Edward Granton could start to cash in assets, to try and get back on an even keel, but he would be risking not just failing to make a profit on his original investment but taking a loss, as well.

No, all that could keep Granton plc—and Granton himself—afloat was a white knight.

Was Kazandros Corp going to be that white knight? He would know soon enough, thought Nikos. But it would be on *his* terms, not Edward Granton's.

This was his baby. His father had handed it to him, had trusted him to make the right call, the one that would pay off in the long term. If the figures performed on the bottom line it might just be a shrewd investment, giving Kazandros Corp a good foothold in the London commercial property market—but even if the figures stacked, there was still substantial risk.

Definitely time to crunch the numbers. Eyes focussed entirely on the printouts Edward Granton was putting in front of him, Nikos blanked out the rest of the world.

Including the peach of a girl who was Edward Granton's too-young daughter.

Sophie studied her reflection critically. More critically than she'd done since—oh, she couldn't remember when! It was probably when she'd started going out with Joel, but that had been over a year ago, and he was long gone. It was funny, she thought now, examining whether her eye make-up was exactly even on both sides, that she'd ever been keen on Joel. Oh, he had obvious charms—blond, good-looking, popular…

But he was just a boy. She stilled a moment, eyes widening unconsciously as she stared at herself.

Nikos Kazandros wasn't a boy. Yet again his image formed in her head. It seemed to have imprinted itself on her instantly, indelibly, and every time she called it up she felt her pulse give a little flurry. It was a gorgeous feeling. It made her feel a funny mix of excited and shivery, as well. She'd never felt like that about Joel, that was for sure! More a sort of satisfaction that he'd chosen *her* to go out with instead of another girl, Hayley. Her eyes darkened briefly. Not that he hadn't gone straight out with Hayley after she and he had split…

She tightened her mouth. Yes, well, Hayley had made it clear she was more than eager to give Joel what he wanted from his girlfriends! What he'd wanted from her, too, but hadn't got. Hence the split.

Her mouth pressed tighter. No way would she ever have dreamt of wasting the occasion on Joel who, with hindsight, had obviously only gone out with her to try and get her into bed. Nothing special—just one more conquest for him.

Well, it's not going to be like that! It's going to be something really, really special—someone really, really special!

Without volition, the imprint of her father's business guest formed in her head again. Immediately she blinked, telling herself it was to test her mascara was not running. But she knew it was to counter the sudden quiver that ran through her as she put the two thoughts together.

Someone special.

And Nikos Kazandros.

She pulled back from the mirror. No—that was absurd!

She'd only just set eyes on the man, spent a bare few minutes in his company. And now here she was thinking—

She felt herself colour, and stood up from her dressing stool. She was being ridiculous. She took a step backwards, moving to inspect her whole appearance, focussing only on that.

She had, she knew, pulled out all the stops.

But for Nikos Kazandros a woman would have to!

With looks like his—not to mention the flash car and his obviously wealthy background!—Nikos Kazandros wouldn't even have to crook his little finger to get girls flocking around him! They'd all be as breathless as she'd been.

Again she felt her heart-rate quicken, felt her lungs take in a swift, shallow breath. Felt that gorgeous little shivery feeling flutter through her. Excitement caught at her. She took one last look at her reflection. If she couldn't make Nikos Kazandros look twice at her now, she never would!

What if he does? The voice sounded in her head. Yes, Nikos Kazandros was gorgeous—two hundred percent, twenty-two carat gorgeous—but he was their dinner guest, that was all.

Then you'd better make the most of him, hadn't you? The voice sounded again, but it was a different one this time. One that made her glance at the slim gold watch around her wrist, and then, flicking her hair back off her shoulders, trot to the door and set off downstairs.

She could hear her father's voice from the drawing room. The doors were open this time, and yet for a moment, breath catching, she paused in the threshold. She didn't do it deliberately. It was because she was suddenly breathless.

Nervous.

Maybe he's not as gorgeous as I thought. Maybe when I see him again I'll be disappointed. Think his nose too big, his eyes too close-set. See flaws in him. Change my mind over him.

But that wasn't the only reason she was nervous, she knew. There was another reason—one to do with a sudden deep sense that she was standing on the threshold of something significant.

Deliberately, quite deliberately as she walked into the room, she did not do what every instinct was trying to compel her to do and let her eyes go to the tall, dark figure standing across the room. She could see him at the periphery of her vision, but she wouldn't let her eyes fly to him.

Her father was greeting her warmly. Almost as if he were relieved at her arrival. The disquieting thought distracted her. She went up and kissed him on the cheek, then turned to their guest.

'Mr Kazandros.' She smiled.

For a moment he didn't answer her smile. For a moment his face was expressionless. Sophie found herself wondering at it. Then, as if a switch had been thrown, he was greeting her in return.

'Miss Granton.' He gave a small bow of his head, very foreign. It reminded her of Vienna, where everyone had seemed so formal all the time. She gave a light laugh.

'Oh, please, do call me Sophie. Miss Granton makes me sound like someone in Jane Austen! Probably a maiden aunt.'

Something moved in his eyes. 'Unlikely,' he said, his voice very dry.

But she wasn't paying a great deal of attention. As she'd let her gaze go to him, to greet him, exhilaration had swept through her. She hadn't been imagining it! He really was as drop-dead, gulpingly gorgeous as she'd first thought! How could she even have thought there might be any flaws? There were none—absolutely none! He really, really was just shiveringly fantastic!

And he definitely was no boy. This was a man—a man who moved through the world, doing business, driving incredible cars, sophisticated, assured, skilled, experienced.

Experienced.

The word repeated itself in her head. With connotations that made her breath tighter. She found her eyes moving to his mouth.

Sculpted, mobile.

Experienced.

She felt heat beat up in her throat. *He'd know how to kiss fantastically...*

Her father was saying something, and she forced herself to listen.

'Your usual orange juice, pet?'

He was crossing over to the drinks cabinet against the other wall. She took a little breath.

'Oh, I think I'll have a Bellini tonight, please, Daddy.' Immediately she wished she hadn't said 'Daddy' like that.

It makes me sound like a little girl.

She didn't look at Nikos Kazandros in case she saw the thought in his eyes. She didn't want him to think of her as a little girl.

Her father paused by the cabinet. 'Sophie, pet, there's no champagne open. I don't want to waste a bottle on a single drink. Have something else.'

She was momentarily stymied. Then she recovered. She looked back at Nikos Kazandros. He had that veiled look on his face again.

'What are you drinking, Mr Kazandros?' she asked, eyeing his shallow glass, which he was holding with long, square-tipped fingers. Her voice had a breathless touch to it.

She could see the switch being thrown again. The veiled look was gone.

'Nikos,' he said softly, as if he were speaking only to her. 'If I am to call you Sophie.' A smile, tantalisingly brief, as was the quiver that it engendered in her, hovered at the corner of one mouth. 'And I am having a martini—very dry. It is an…acquired taste.'

'Sophie, you'd hate it, believe me,' said her father from the drinks cabinet.

'A sweet martini can be very palatable,' suggested Nikos.

She smiled. 'Perfect!' she said. 'There you go, Daddy. A sweet martini for me, please!'

Oh, damn, she'd said 'Daddy' again, and again her gaze flicked to Nikos Kazandros—no, *Nikos,* she amended, and felt a little thrill, as if of triumph—to see whether he thought her childish. But the veiled look was back on his face. She wondered at it, but at the same time realised she was glad of it, too, because it seemed to give her the opportunity to look at him, as she wanted to, without actually falling headfirst into his gaze, because his eyes were not quite meeting hers.

But they were on her face, though. And more than her face. They'd flicked downwards, she could see—only for an instant, but it was enough. Enough to tell her, again with a little thrill of triumph, that she had not pulled out all the stops in vain.

The peach-coloured cocktail dress she wore was one of her very favourites. There was something about the colour that just absolutely suited her skin tone and her hair. The material was so light it skimmed her body, but outlined it, as well. It wasn't at all overtly revealing—but somehow it seemed to indicate an awful lot. The hem was a little way above her knees, yet it lengthened the line of her legs incredibly. The bodice was not tight, but she knew it gave her a very flattering bust, and made her waist look even more slender than it was.

It had been incredibly expensive, even for her budget, but because she loved it so she got good value from it, wearing it over and over again.

But never so gratefully as now.

Now, as Nikos Kazandros's experienced eyes flicked over her—*how many women had he looked over to judge whether they were good enough to interest him?*—she knew, with every ingrained feminine instinct, that what he saw he liked.

Liked a lot.

Her lips parted, and her smile was one of mingled gladness—and relief.

I want him to like me.

He was a world away from her. Not just because she was still a student, and he was a man old enough to be doing business with her father, but because, for all her more-than-comfortable existence, it was obvious just from looking at him that Nikos Kazandros's stalking ground was the kind of glamorous watering holes that littered the Mediterranean and the Caribbean, the Alps and the Indian Ocean islands. Fashionable clubs in fashionable cities, with the kind of exclusive membership that filtered out anyone not sufficiently rich, sufficiently sophisticated. The world of serious money and serious spending. That was the world Nikos Kazandros belonged to.

For a moment she felt dismay fill her, knowing the distance between them was too great.

Then his eyes flicked back up to meet hers again.

The veil was gone. And in its place—

Sophie's breath stilled in her body. Completely. As if oxygen were no longer necessary to her survival.

Because it wasn't. The only thing necessary to her survival at this moment was the look that Nikos Kazandros was pouring into her eyes.

She had heard the expression 'the world stopped turning'—now she and knew what it meant. For one incredible, timeless moment she just gazed back at him. Feeling everything stop.

Then, from a long way away, she heard her father's voice. 'Sophie?'

She blinked. The world started again. Her father was there, holding out her sweet martini to her. She took it and dipped her head, wanting only to take a large gulp of the drink.

There was heat in her throat, and not from the alcohol. From a different source of intoxication. Far, far more powerful.

Powerful enough to sweep her away, for ever, into a different world, from which she knew, with a strange, vague sense of fatality, she might never, never return.

And from which she knew she would never want to.

Slowly, she raised the glass to her lips, as if toasting that fate. Her eyes went back to his. They were veiled again, but she knew why now. Didn't mind. She smiled, lips parting over pearled teeth.

Nikos took a mouthful of his own dry martini. He could do with it. Self-control was slamming down hard over him and he needed to regain it, urgently.

Hell, if he'd thought Sophie Granton a peach when he'd first seen her, with her hair flying and almond blossom drifting on her gypsy clothes, now he couldn't even begin to find the right description for her.

Except—knockout.

But not in the way the women in his world usually earned that soubriquet. Not from wearing the kind of gown that stunned male libidos a kilometre wide. Sophie Granton's impact as she'd stood in the doorway a few minutes ago had been quite different. Hitting him in a quite different place. One where he'd never been hit before.

And in one he had, as well.

That dress she was wearing and the sleek, groomed fall of

hair had hit a spot that was very, very familiar to him. The spot that had, right over the top of it, a great big *D* for *Desire.*

He knew he shouldn't even begin to indulge it, but that was easier said than done. Hell, it was impossible to do! The way she stood there, with her perfect figure, perfect face, perfect hair. Now, with make-up on, she looked older, he realised, and realised too that he was glad of it.

Because maybe this peach of a girl wasn't out of bounds, after all?

A reality check crashed through his brain. He wasn't here to run around with Edward Granton's knockout daughter, he was here to find out whether Granton plc would be worth the trouble and risk rescuing it entailed. That was all.

And yet—

Well, he was here for dinner and he would make the most of it. Make the most of appreciating this beautiful golden girl.

The discussion with Edward Granton had not been easy. The numbers did not look as if they were going to crunch well—the only question was, did it put the company out of play or not? It would be a tricky call to make.

Granton himself was looking strained. That in itself was a bad sign, a revealing one. He knew that his financial survival depended on a rescue. Of course Granton might have other white knights in the offing, but any intimation that he had could also be a bluff and a gamble. Nikos's father had taught him about the business world well, and that any mistake could cost him dearly. His father had raised him never to be a rich man's son, thinking money came easily. No matter how large and financially sound Kazandros Corp was now, it could always be lost... No, whatever happened, he would make the right call about Granton plc—his father was trusting him to do that.

And he certainly trusted him enough not to get diverted by anything other than the task he'd been sent to London to do.

Including this girl he couldn't take his eyes from. For a moment he toyed with coming up with some excuse to get out of dinner. Maybe he should. It would be safer.

Safer?

The word repeated itself in his head. Why had it come to him? He frowned mentally. It made it sound as if there was some sort of danger ahead. He brushed it aside impatiently. He was overreacting. All he was going to do was have dinner with Edward Granton and his daughter.

Did she know how precarious her father's position was? How shaky the financial edifice that kept her in designer clothes and living in this house in one of London's most expensive districts? Not to mention paid her student fees and bought her the grand piano he could see in the room behind this one?

No, she couldn't possibly. Not only did Edward Granton strike him as very much the old-fashioned type of father—indulgent and protective—but she herself had an absolutely carefree air about her. The only thing on her mind—and Nikos noted it with a satisfaction that surprised him with its intensity—was himself.

It was completely obvious to him. Oh, she wasn't making a play for him or giving him any kind of come-on—it wasn't that at all. So what was it?

She was entirely natural in her reaction to him.

He could see it in her eyes, the way she gazed at him, meeting his gaze and revelling in it, lips slightly parted, the light, slightly breathless voice.

He couldn't but respond to her.

'The name Holland Park comes from Holland House, which used to stand in the park itself,' she was saying. 'Sadly, the house was bombed in the war, and there's only fragments left, like the Orangery. But the park is beautiful, and I always walk through it on my way back from college if the weather is fine, like today.'

'And arrive covered in almond blossom.' He smiled.

'It's glorious this time of year, isn't it?' She smiled back.

He found himself stilling again, the way he'd done when he'd seen her posed, paused, in the doorway. Her smile was as breathtaking as she was—more than breathtaking. Enchanting.

Enchanting…

The word floated in his mind. Where had it come from? He didn't know, but now that it was there he knew with a certainty he didn't even think of questioning that it was the right word for her.

What is she doing to me?

The question flickered, unanswered. Unanswerable.

And anyway he didn't care right now what she was doing to him—only that she was doing it.

And she went right on doing it all through the evening. Smiling her radiant smile at him, gazing wide-eyed at him, making no secret at all of what she was doing. And it didn't repel him, or annoy him, or make him cynical, or any such thing. Instead he simply…reciprocated.

I've never met a girl like her.

The words took shape in his head and he knew they were true. He went on thinking them all through the meal, during which the conversation was predominantly between him and Sophie. When they went to the drawing room for coffee Nikos remembered what Edward Granton had said in the afternoon, and asked Sophie if she would play something for them on the piano. To the music he was largely indifferent—but to the pianist he was anything but. What he wanted was to watch her, poised at the instrument, her beautiful profile outlined for him against the glorious fall of her pale silken hair, her hands moving delicately, expertly over the ivory keys. He sat, coffee cup resting in his hand, eyes very slightly narrowed, focussed with absolute intensity on Sophie Granton's exquisite face.

Knowing with complete certainty that whatever happened he had to see her again.

He showed his hand when the evening finally ended. As he took his leave, still feeling her starry gaze upon him, he smiled down at her.

'Will you allow me to take you to a concert while I am in London?' he murmured and then, throwing an appropriate glance at Edward Granton, 'With your father's permission, of course?'

For a moment it seemed to him the man hesitated. Then, as he looked at his daughter briefly, he nodded. Nikos could see that Sophie's eyes were shining like stars.

'That would be lovely!' she exclaimed.

A thrill ran through her. He wanted to see her again! He'd asked her out! This gorgeous, incredible man who simply took her breath away was interested in her! He had to be— he wouldn't have asked her to go to a concert with him otherwise. He'd just have said goodnight and gone, and that would have been that.

But he wants to see me again!

As her father showed her guest out, Sophie flung her arms around herself and gave herself a huge, disbelieving hug. A few moments later her father came back into the drawing room.

'Oh, Daddy, isn't he *wonderful!*'

There was a slightly strange expression on her father's face. 'He's a very good-looking young man,' he said.

She read his expression, and answered it with a wry one

of her own. 'That's not a compliment—it's a warning, isn't it?' she said.

He gave a reluctant nod, then took a breath. 'Nikos Kazandros is very clearly the kind of privileged young man, with his looks and the lifestyle he leads, who will have good reason to expect that females will fall at his feet! And,' he added, 'to expect that they will do what he wants them to do!' He looked straight at her. 'Be careful, Sophie. I would hate you to get hurt. And especially now, when—'

He stopped. As if silencing himself deliberately. Then he changed the subject. 'It's been a long day. I've meetings first thing tomorrow, so I may not see you before you set off for college.' He came to kiss her goodnight, on each cheek. 'Forgive me for being over-protective, my darling. I only ever want what is best for you. Enjoy going out with Mr Kazandros, if you are set on it. But don't expect too much of it. And, Sophie?' His tone changed again. 'Remember that I may be doing business with him.' There was a tightness in his voice suddenly, and Sophie stepped back, looking at him a moment.

'Is…is it important business?' she asked hesitantly.

The tight look was back on his face. Then she saw it relax. 'Just don't give away any trade secrets!' he said, with deliberate lightness.

She put on another wry smile. 'I don't know any!'

Her father's expression flickered for a moment—as if, she thought, he weren't quite sure about something. Then he nodded. 'Just as well.' He dropped a last kiss on her forehead.

But as he did she felt his hands tighten on her shoulders suddenly, as if emotion were going through him. She felt a wave of her filial love seize her, coming on top of the state of exhilaration that had been mounting all evening.

'Oh, Daddy, I'll be careful! Careful of everything! Careful

of letting out trade secrets and of letting him sweep me away! But, oh, *oh*, he is just *so* wonderful!' She stepped away, skipping down the stairs on feet as light as air, her mind totally absorbed once more with the wonderful, glorious, breathtaking gorgeousness of Nikos Kazandros!

The next day was an agony. She so wanted to phone home, to find out if he'd called with a concert date, but made herself wait until she got back from college.

To find no message waiting for her.

Her heart plunged. Had he just said that about the concert but not meant it? She dragged herself up to her room, sank down on her bed, feeling her heart sinking with her. Blankly she stared. Had she really thought he would ask her out?

Yes—yes, I did! I really did!

She felt her insides clench, and for a moment it was like a physical pain, knowing that she'd been so ridiculously optimistic. Her hands clutched in her lap as she stared down at the carpet, knowing with a heavy, bleak certainty that she would never hear from Nikos Kazandros again. Never, ever, ever…

The house phone by her bedside rang, and listlessly she picked it up.

'Miss Sophie?' Mrs T's brisk, tart tones came down the line. 'I'd appreciate it if you came down to the kitchen. There's been a delivery for you, and it's not the sort of thing I can be running up and down to the top floor with!'

My music books, thought Sophie dully. She had some on order, and they weighed a ton, so she knew why Mrs T was reluctant to bring them up herself. Dolefully, she trailed downstairs. But when she saw what was on the dresser, elation soared through her again.

Flowers—a bouquet so vast she knew exactly why the

housekeeper hadn't tried to carry them, their rich, exotic fragrance pouring through the room. And with them a note. Handwritten.

I hope a Covent Garden gala will be acceptable to you?
I'll send a car for seven tomorrow.

It was just signed 'NK'.

She hugged it to her and danced all the way back up to her rooms, the blooms in her grip wobbling precariously, her heart singing with delirious delight.

If she'd taken for ever to get ready just for dinner, for the following evening she took all afternoon. She was ready—just—when the sleek limo drew up outside the house, and though she felt a stab of disappointment when she realised she was the only passenger, she could feel her excitement mounting as the car made its slow way towards Covent Garden. By the time she was disgorged she was trembling, and as she climbed out, Nikos was walking forward.

She froze.

He was wearing evening dress, and if she'd thought he looked gorgeous in a lounge suit, in a tuxedo he simply melted her on the spot!

He took her hand, murmuring something in Greek. His eyes were fixed on her, and she felt the thrill come again.

'You look…' he said, but there was a husk in his voice and he could not finish.

There weren't words to describe her! Oh, he could describe the dress—a slim column of ivory silk—and a matching stole, picked out with the most delicate embroidery, and around her throat pearls like angel's tears. Her hair was caught in a loose coil at the nape of her neck, and her make-up was so barely there that it seemed invisible, except for the exquisite enhancement of her beauty. A beauty he could find no words for, only desire.

Oh, not desire as he knew it, but a new, different kind of desire that had nothing in common with the emotion he usually associated with the term. No, this was a new kind of sensation. One that made him want to…want to…

He didn't know what. And didn't bother to try and find words. What for? He didn't need them. Didn't need anything right now except to smile at her and lead her forward into the opera house, thronged with arrivals, and murmur something appropriate about being glad that she'd wanted to come this evening.

Her eyes widened. 'Glad? I can't even believe you got tickets! They're gold-dust for events like this!'

The corner of his mouth pulled. 'Ah, so that's why you accepted my invitation. And there I was, being a conceited idiot and hoping it was for my sake, not a gold-dust ticket to a gala!'

Her eyes flew to him. 'How could you think that?' she breathed.

He stilled. He seemed to do that all the time. She kept stopping him in his tracks. She'd done it over and over again the evening before, but now, like this, as she gazed at him he felt it again, like a trip hammer, slamming down on him.

What is she doing to me?

He became aware they were holding up others, and jolted forwards again, guiding her smoothly. But he didn't touch her. His hand hovered behind her back, but somehow he felt that the kind of casual body contact he would take for granted with any other woman would be out of place.

When I touch her, it will be special…

And this evening would be special, he knew. Not just because even for him it had taken considerable effort—not to say expense!—to get hold of tickets for the evening, but because—well, *because*, that was all.

He stopped analysing. Gave himself to the experience. The experience of feeling that something was happening to him that was new—quite, quite new.

She was walking gracefully forward, and he could see male eyes turning. And he could also see that she was gazing around her as they made their way through the throng, her eyes widening every now and then. In the crush bar, champagne was circulating, and Nikos took a glass for himself and for her. She took a sip, then leant forward, slightly towards him.

He was raising his glass. 'To a memorable evening,' he said.

She didn't need to echo his words to know that they were true. Wonderfully, magically true!

And they stayed true all evening. She sat beside him in the plush seats, her face alight, as some of the greatest artists in the world sang on the famous stage below, wreathed in its crimson velvet curtains. All the time, every moment of the gala, she was overpoweringly conscious of Nikos sitting beside her—the lean strength of his body, the occasional breath-catching brush of his sleeve, even though she kept her hands clasped in her lap. By the time the gala ended her emotions were sky-high, swept up by the soaring music and artistry of the performers. In the final applause she turned to Nikos.

'Thank you! *Thank you!* All my life I'll remember this evening!'

Her eyes were like stars, dewed with emotion.

She saw his face still again, as it had done before. Then, slowly, he reached for her hand and raised it to his lips.

'As will I,' he said softly.

She could only sit, her heart soaring, face alight, lips parted, gazing at him, feeling more than she had ever felt in her life before! More than she had ever thought it possible to feel.

The soft brush of his lips on her hand had made her breathless, and then he was lowering her hand, but not relinquishing it, instead drawing her to her feet as the audience started to get to theirs. She felt his fingers lace through hers, so strong, so warm, holding hers, and felt faint with the wonderfulness of it.

Nikos! His name reverberated in her head. *Nikos! Nikos! Nikos!*

She floated on air as she walked beside him, his fingers still laced with hers, as they made their slow procession from the opera house. Leaving took ages, because the narrow streets outside were thronged, but eventually Nikos was handing her into the limo, and she was sinking into its depths, he was coming in beside her, and the limo was moving slowly off.

'I asked your father if I might take you for supper after the performance,' Nikos said. His eyes glinted. 'I've got you till midnight, but you must be home on the stroke of twelve!'

She gave a little gurgle of laughter. 'He's terribly Victorian.'

But Nikos did not laugh with her. 'He is right to be careful of you,' he said soberly. Then his tone altered. 'Now, I hope my choice of restaurant will please you.'

He could have suggested fish and chips and she would have been enchanted, but where he took her was infinitely more salubrious. It was uncrowded and, best of all, their table was very private. What she ate she had no idea, nor did she have much more idea what they talked about. Sophie knew her whole attention was on Nikos—Nikos alone! Gazing at him, smiling at him, listening to him, knowing with every passing moment that he was the most wonderful, wonderful man she had ever met! And by the time, two hours later, he reluctantly escorted her from the limo up to the front door of her father's house, she knew something else, as well. Something even more precious.

She was in love.

She knew it for a certainty—irrefutably, incontestably. She was in love with Nikos Kazandros!

Dreamily, she waltzed around her room, knowing she was happier than she had ever been in her life, and that the rest of her life was going to be the most wonderful in the world—because she was in love with Nikos Kazandros! In love! In love! *In love!*

And nothing could stop it! Nothing!

CHAPTER THREE

'SOPHIE.'

The sound of her name was like a rasp across wounded flesh. For a moment filled with agony Sophie felt the pain of it. Then, steeling herself, she turned expressionless eyes on Nikos.

'What do you want?' she responded stonily.

Something moved—flashed—in those dark eyes into whose depths she had once fallen and drowned.

'Want?' he echoed. The taunt was still there, the harshness. 'Why should I want anything—anything that you have to offer now? Cosmo's welcome to your well-displayed charms!' The eyes lashed over her, the whip of contempt laying bare her skin.

But she would not feel it, would not feel the lash of his words, his taunting. What was it to her? What was *he* to her?

Nothing. Nothing at all, ever again!

'Get lost, Nikos,' she said, and turned away, plunging into the melee in the room. Even Cosmo Dimistris seemed like a haven from this unbearable encounter.

As he watched her walk away through the room, Nikos felt emotion sear through him. Then, abruptly, it was overridden. He suddenly realised he could no longer see Georgias. Cursing under his breath, he stared around, as if he could conjure him up, and then, a grim look on his face, he headed down a wide corridor that clearly led towards the apartment's bedrooms.

It took him a while to find his charge, throwing open one door after another and finding the rooms occupied. He carried on his furious search until he found Georgias, his tie loose, shirt undone, the girl he'd been dancing with even more undressed, the pair of them collapsed on a bed together.

Nikos wrested her off, ignoring her squeals of inebriated protest at being balked of her prey, then yanked Georgias upright. He was almost completely out of it, his eyes glazed, hair tousled. Nikos hoped to God it was merely alcohol in his system.

It took a while to get Georgias out of the apartment, their way barred by the milling party throng and imprecations not to leave, and Georgias had a suddenly reanimated desire to dance again, but finally Nikos manhandled him out, and down in the lift.

Getting him across the lobby required some force, but once the night air hit, Georgias collapsed almost completely. Nikos glared angrily out across the roadway. Rain was sluicing down, cold and soaking, but at least a taxi driver had seen him sheltering under the portico of the luxury apartment block, and was diverting towards him. With effort, Nikos manhandled Georgias inside, and thrust him into the far corner of the cab, where he slumped in an ungainly fashion, his eyes closing in insensible stupor. Nikos gritted his teeth.

Brusquely, he gave the name of their hotel, and the cabbie nodded and moved off, tyres sluicing through the rain-filled gutter. Nikos threw himself back into his corner of the cab, his mind in turmoil. Only one image dominated it.

Sophie Granton.

He felt emotion surge inside him again—convulsing, turbid. Filled with anger, with more than anger.

Why the hell did I have to see her?

Why the hell had she had to rise up from the pit like that? Seeing her again, seeing what she'd come to—her dress half hanging off her, keeping company with the likes of jerks like Cosmo!

Memory slanted through his head, unwanted, unbidden— but vivid.

Her graceful body sheathed in a column of ivory, a chiffon stole around her pale shoulders, her face radiant with a beauty that had made his breath stop in his lungs, stepping towards him from the limo to where he waited for her outside the opera house, and her eyes, luminescent, glowing—fixed on him...

With brute force, he twisted his head away, banishing the memory. Now, instead, the last memory he would ever have of her would be draped on Cosmo Dimistris's arm at a party for coke-heads and tarts....

His mouth thinned, tightened to a whiplash, a lash that flayed across his soul. If that was what she wanted now, that was what she could have.

And yet—

Abruptly, he leant forward, rapping on the glass behind the driver. The cab slowed and the cabbie twisted slightly, sliding open the partition.

'Turn around,' said Nikos.

Sophie was walking. It was raining, she was soaked, she was freezing, but she didn't care. Not about that, but about how stupid she'd been.

No, not just stupid. That was far, far too weak a word. Anger raged inside her. At herself. Sickening, gut-churning. It was like acid inside her. Eating her up.

Will I never, ever learn? Will I go on being so insanely, criminally stupid—so pathetically, abjectly naïve?

Virulent self-hatred snaked through her.

I thought I'd finally learnt my lessons! All of them! I thought I could finally say that I'd wised up!

Like hell she had! The needles of freezing rain pounded down on her and she welcomed them as the punishment she deserved. She walked on blindly, writhing in self-loathing and bleak rage.

In the roadway, a car turned. A cab, she realised too late, as it arced through the wash of water in the gutter, sending a plume of cold, dirty water over her legs.

'Get in.'

The voice was terse. It sounded angry. She stared. The passenger door of the taxi had opened just in front of her, and holding it open was Nikos Kazandros.

'I said get in!'

She froze. And in that moment Nikos reached out and grabbed at her. For an instant she resisted, but he was far too strong for her, and he pulled her into the cab, thrusting her down on to the jump seat opposite him, yanking the cab door shut.

'OK, drive,' he said to the cabbie. The cabbie glanced briefly at his latest passenger, but she was just sitting there, making no move to get out, so he let out the throttle and moved off in to the traffic again.

On her seat, Sophie felt her brain start to work again. And her muscles. She started to shiver, violently. Water was running down from the hair plastered wetly to her head.

'Are you mad?' Nikos heard himself grind out to Sophie. 'Walking along looking like that?'

She stared at him through rain-wet eyelashes. Her mascara was starting to run. It looked like black tears.

'I didn't have a coat with me,' she said. Her teeth were starting to chatter, and she had to clench her jaw to stop them.

'And you didn't think to take a taxi?' Nikos retorted witheringly. In the shifting light of the interior of the cab he could see the soaked satin of her dress outline every contour of her body. Her evening gown was clinging to her like a second skin, and twice as revealing. She looked half naked…

Involuntarily, he felt, to his own anger and self-disgust, an awareness of her body beneath the semi-transparent material. Of the twin swell of her breasts, their nipples standing out from the cold. He dragged his eyes back to her face.

She made no answer to his jibe, only closed her mouth tightly, jaw clamped. She was shivering, Nikos could see, and clutching a tiny bag on her lap. He pulled his gaze away, deliberately glancing at Georgias. But Georgias was slumped into stertorous sleep in the corner of the cab.

'There's a tube station! Let me out!'

Nikos's attention was whipped back again. Sophie was rapping on the glass behind the cabbie's seat, and he started to slow down as they approached the station. Nikos's anger mounted.

'Are you insane? You can't go on the tube like that! You're half naked!' His eyes flashed darkly. 'What the hell are you doing, anyway? You were with Cosmo.'

She didn't answer him, just started to fumble with the door catch as the taxi pulled over beside the entrance to the tube station. Nikos's hand laced out and imprisoned her wrist.

'I asked you a question—'

'Get lost.' Her voice was a low snarl. 'I'm getting out here.'

'The hell you are!' He rapped on the cabbie's glass. 'Keep going!'

The cabbie shrugged and set off again, but Nikos could see him glancing in his rearview mirror. He slid the glass partition open.

'I'm giving her a lift, that's all. You can drop me off at my hotel, and I'll pay the fare for wherever she wants to go. That OK with you?' he finished witheringly.

The cabbie eyed him, then nodded. 'Whatever you say, guv. If the lady don't object.'

Nikos's gaze ripped back to Sophie. She was sitting there, hunched, arms half crossed across her torso now, as if to veil her body from him. She was still shivering, staring expressionlessly at the floor. Her face was blank. Quite blank. Water from her sodden hair still dripped down the line of her jaw. Mascara ran down her cheeks. She looked a mess.

Why wasn't she with Cosmo? Nikos lurched back into his seat, eyes on her. 'So, did Cosmo give you the push?'

She didn't answer, only gave him a brief, knifing glance before closing in on herself again. Her blankness angered Nikos. Everything about her angered him. Everything. He could feel his anger rising—biting. Wanting to find an out.

'Or did you change your mind about putting out for him? Is that it?'

That got a reaction. Eyes like daggers flashed up at him, fury in them.

'That wasn't ever on the table! Nor, for your information, did I *choose* his company!'

'So how come you ended up with him?' Nikos pushed back.

The flash in the eyes came again. 'He hired me for the evening! As an escort.'

Nikos stilled, not believing what he'd just heard her say. 'A *hooker?*'

'I am *not* a hooker!' The snarl came from her throat. 'I took a job at an *escort* agency, as an *escort*! That's *all*! I'm well aware that some girls do a hell of a lot more than just have dinner and drinks with their clients, but *not me*!' Breath razored in her lungs as her eyes blazed. 'So whatever else you think, and whatever else that disgusting jerk thought, that was *all* I signed up for! And *he* knew it, and the *agency* knew it, and now *you* can know it too—and you can take it and *choke* on it!'

She was fumbling for the door catch again, dimly aware, in the fury and tumult in her head, that the taxi had stopped. She couldn't find the catch, and then, as she fumbled desperately, she felt a hand close over hers, pulling it away. The cabbie was speaking, opening the partition slightly, his voice wary. 'You OK there, luv?'

'She's fine!' Nikos cut across roughly, closing the glass again. 'Keep driving!'

For a moment longer the cabbie looked over his shoulder. But Sophie was sitting frozen again, as if all the fire had been doused with a pail of water. Oh, what the *hell*? she thought, a bitter weariness crushing down on her as the cold in her bones took over and she started to shiver again.

Why did I rise to it? What do I care what he thinks of me? What could I possibly, possibly care? He's nothing to me— nothing, nothing, nothing.

Depression, weariness, and despair like a deadweight crushed her down. Her shivering intensified. Her mind seemed like a blur, a mush. Too much had happened, too much overload. She could not take any more…

'Sophie—'

Nikos's voice cut across her deadening mind, and she raised blurred eyes to him. Her make-up was running into them, stinging, and drops of rain were still oozing down her forehead, making her blink.

Nikos. I'm in a taxi with Nikos Kazandros, and I don't know why, or how, or what the hell is going on, and I just can't cope any more, I can't…can't cope…

'Sophie!' Nikos spoke again, louder this time. Demanding attention. She stared at him and realised he had taken off his jacket, was holding it out to her. She shrank back, as if it were poisoned.

'I don't want it,' she bit out. 'I'm fine.'

'You're soaking wet and freezing—even in here.'

'I'm fine,' she repeated doggedly.

Nikos's dark eyes glinted balefully, but he shrugged himself back into his jacket. 'You *really* believed Cosmo Dimistris just wanted a sexy female to have dinner with?' The question was scathing.

She said nothing, only clenched her jaw.

'Answer me!'

Her eyes flashed again. 'What do you want to know for? What possible concern is it of yours?'

'Just tell me,' he gritted.

'Yes,' she enunciated, berating herself even as she did so, because she owed this man no explanation, no justification. But she wanted to wipe the sneer from his face—needed to. 'I did. Because that is what I signed up to. When I went to the agency, I said I would only do dinner dates, nothing else. And the woman said fine, it was up to me, it was my choice, and the agency didn't get involved with anything more than providing the introduction—'

His laugh, harsh and short, cut across her. '*Introduction*? Did you think you were working for a *dating* agency? No one can be that naïve!'

She twisted her head away. A rock was in her stomach. Yes, she'd been that naïve, all right. So naïve—right up to the moment when she'd gone to find Cosmo Dimistris and he had offered her some cocaine, having clearly just snorted some himself, and said it would make the sex much, much better, whilst steering her into a bedroom.

The rock in her stomach hardened, and she felt again the lash of self-hatred that she'd flagellated herself with as she'd trudged down the rain-sluiced street. Cosmo had made it savagely clear to her, with a laugh so coarse that it had almost obliterated the hot groping of his hand, that if she wasn't going to come up with the goods, she could stop wasting his time and get the hell out, because there were plenty of other girls here who would provide what he wanted.

The taxi was turning off the road, heading into the sweeping entrance of a hotel.

'Your hotel, guv.'

The voice of the cabbie penetrated her self-castigation. Immediately she made for the door. She had to get out, and fast. Out and away. Away from Nikos Kazandros.

'Stay where you are.' His voice was harsh, and it was clearly an order.

She glowered at him.

'The cab will take you wherever you want to go. I'll settle the fare to cover it.'

He was turning his attention now to the other occupant of the cab. Sophie had no idea who he was, and cared less. She just wanted Nikos gone, *gone*. And then she could get the hell out of here.

Wordlessly, Nikos set about the task of making Georgias sufficiently conscious to get out of the cab. He could feel the thrum of the humming engine of the car as it hovered under the portico of the Park Lane hotel.

'Out,' he said brusquely to Georgias, thrusting him on to the concourse, where he stood swaying and blinking. He turned to climb out himself, then paused, looking one last time at Sophie as she sat there hunched, still shivering. One final question seared through his brain. His eyes bored into her as he leant towards her.

'Why? Give me one good reason *why*? Whatever the hell you are—hooker, escort, good-time girl, whatever—why go anywhere near this…this *sleaze*? Take a good, hard look at yourself when you get home—a good, hard look, Sophie— and think about whether you like what you see. Ask yourself why you're doing what you're doing.'

His voice was low, audible only to her. Her eyes flashed up, and for a second, just a second, Nikos felt himself reeling as if she had physically struck him.

'Why do you *think*?' she bit out, hissing, like Medusa's snakes. 'I need the bloody money!'

Her face was contorted, her eyes like daggers, ringed with black mascara, like black hollows, and in that instant Nikos recoiled, as if seeing a death's head. Then his face set and he hurled himself from the cab, slamming the door, pausing only to extract his wallet and, with grim, tight face, thrust a fifty-pound note at the cabbie.

'Take her wherever she wants,' he said. Then he seized Georgias by the arm and marched him into the hotel.

Inside the taxi, Sophie stared after him for one long, last moment, until he had disappeared. Then she started to get out of the cab.

'Oi, luv, your fare's covered,' said the cabbie, sliding open his partition.

'I need an Underground station,' she said, in a low, strained voice.

The cabbie looked concerned. 'Luv, he's right. You can't go on a train all wet the way you are. You'll get attacked. Mugged. Or worse. Look…' He shrugged his shoulders. 'It's not my business, but I'd be happier taking you somewhere. I don't want to read about you in the paper tomorrow, OK?'

He didn't wait for an answer, just started the cab moving again. Sophie went on sitting there, shivering. But it wasn't just the cold that was making her tremble.

The cabbie went on talking, half turning his head to do so. 'Listen, luv, I've got a daughter your age. I wouldn't like to see her—well, in the state you are. And I'd tell her straight what I'm going to tell you.' He took a breath. 'Blokes like that—' he nodded his head back in the direction of the hotel '—they're bad news for girls. All flash and cash and that's your lot. Stay clear of them. That's what I say—and it's what any dad would say. And if you ain't got a dad…well, I'll say it for him—OK? A dad wants to be proud of his daughter—and to know she's safe.'

Sophie heard the words, heard them from very far away. From a life that had gone for ever. That could never come back. Never.

And the bitter, bitter irony of what the cabbie had said made her want to burst into savage, hysterical laughter.

Or into tears that would drown her in their bottomless depths.

Nikos stood by the plate-glass window of his hotel lounge, looking out over the darkness of Hyde Park beyond. His tie was undone, his jacket discarded. One hand was splayed against the chill pane, the other cradling a glass of whisky from the drinks cabinet. His face was dark. Blank. Eyes unseeing.

But he was seeing, all right. Except not what was real. Not what existed any more.

But it never did exist—it never did! The past never was what I thought it was, and it took the narrowest damn escape of my life to realise that!

And thank God he *had* escaped!

He felt an old familiar emotion convulse him. One he had not felt now for a long, long time. He had forcibly banned it from existing, though it had taken all his strength to do so. He knew why it had struck again—knew it was inevitable.

Why had he had to see her again? What malign twist of fate had made it happen?

He took a brooding mouthful of the whisky, feeling its fire burn down his throat. He wanted to numb everything inside him. Wanted the alcohol to shut down all sensation, all thought. All memory.

But it wouldn't work. The memory was still alive, writhing like a pit of snakes in his belly.

And it wasn't just memory inside him. There was something more dangerous, more powerful…

No! I will not allow it! I will not let myself go there! Never, ever again! I cauterised it four years ago—and I will not let it back in! I will not!

His mind slammed into action, exerting every gram of self-discipline.

I will control this! It will not control me!

The mantra gritted through his head, repeating as his fingers pressed tighter still around the curve of the glass. It was vital, essential, to keep control. Because if he failed—

The snakes writhed inside him again, and he slugged back another mouthful of whisky. He wanted to sleep, craved oblivion, but he knew with a thick anger that if he slept it would be worse, far worse, than staying awake. If he slept—he would dream.

Memories he could control. But dreams…

He pushed himself away abruptly from the window, and

ranged restlessly around the room. How the hell had Sophie Granton come to end up working as an escort? His glass stilled even as he started to lift it again to his mouth. The image of her face as she'd flung her stinging answer at him seared in his mind.

'I need the bloody money!'

He'd recoiled—the venom in her voice had been virulent.

Again, his brows snapped together. Why was she so strapped for cash?

What had happened to Sophie Granton since he had discovered what she was really after? Granton plc had gone under. He'd known that—known it was inevitable the moment he'd pulled Kazandros Corp out of the negotiations and gone back to Athens to report that the risks were too great.

And so they had been—but not to Kazandros Corp. Only to himself.

But I cut my losses—I got out in time! I saved my own skin!

But Edward Granton had not been able to save his. The end had come swiftly, his company imploding under the weight of debts, of unrepayable loans, of foreclosures and inevitable financial collapse.

Nikos had been back in Athens then, and what had happened to Edward Granton after his company had gone under had not been Nikos's concern.

Let alone what had happened to his daughter.

So what did happen to her?

Impatiently, he brushed the question aside. Sure, Edward Granton would have had to cut back, would doubtless have taken some face-saving action like opting for early retirement, probably somewhere like Spain. But he was no financial fool, despite having over-extended his company during the recession. He'd have had assets protected from the corporate balance sheet, assets that he could adequately live on, even though it would have meant retrenching.

But maybe Sophie—cosseted as she was by her doting father—hadn't wanted to retrench. Maybe she'd gone on spending money they just didn't have. And maybe now the credit card bills had arrived she thought she'd come up with an easy way to make money to pay them off.

Perhaps she'd really thought that all she had to do was keep a rich man company for the evening and he'd pay for the privilege, not expect anything else in return! A derisive snort broke from Nikos. Well, she'd found out tonight that there was no such thing as easy money! Not that it should have taken more than five minutes with Cosmo to suss that he was in the market for sex, and anything else was just an appetiser. His eyes alone, never mind his wandering hands, should have told her that Cosmo had fully intended her to end up horizontal….

But it was a mistake to let that thought even have house room. Immediately, disastrously, Nikos saw an image from the past flare in his mind…

Sophie, her beauty revealed to him in all its incandescent perfection! Her pearled skin, hair like silk, spread on the pillow like a banner as he took her in his aching arms…

No! With savage rage, he forced the memory out of his head. Tearing it from him as he had once torn Sophie's pleading hands.

His face hardened. Sophie had wanted only one thing from him then, disguise it as she might. The same as she wanted now.

Money. Nothing but money.

Roughly knocking back the last of his whisky, he snapped the glass down on the cabinet.

Enough! He had done with Sophie Granton—she was nothing to him, not any more. And that was all he had to remember!

Face set, he headed for the *en suite* bathroom, and bed.

CHAPTER FOUR

Sophie fumbled with the capsule contained in its silver foil, and managed to extract it. Then with shaking hands, she got it into her mouth and rinsed it down with water from a cracked mug. She wanted the painkiller to work instantly, but knew she would have to wait before the tight, hot pounding in her head would ease and bring relief. If only it could bring a cessation of memory! If only it could erase everything from the night before—*everything*!

Her face contorted. Dear God, how could last night have happened? What vicious twist of fate had heaped that upon her? Four years—*four years*—since her life had been destroyed, and now Nikos Kazandros had reappeared, like some hideous, malign demon, to mock and taunt her in her very hour of desperate self-abasement!

God almighty, did he think she'd *wanted* to take that hideous job? Dressing up like a tart and meeting a complete stranger for the evening? She'd had to force herself to do it! Force herself to let everyone see her in that vulgar, exposing dress, to smile, and make fatuous, feeble conversation to a man who made her flesh crawl, made her feel even dirtier than she felt already.

Hasn't life done enough to me?

The cry came from the depths—the depths where she lived now, to which she had sunk remorselessly, pitilessly.

She stared around her. The tiny, shabby bedsit was hardly big enough for a bed, let alone an alcove with a sink, and a cracked dresser with a hot ring and kettle on it. But it was all she could afford—all she dared afford. She bowed her head, crushed beneath a weight she could not bear.

But she must.

On top of the narrow chest of drawers was the latest letter. Beneath the polite phrase was the harsh, brutal truth.

We regret to inform you that unless the fees are paid in full, in advance, by the end of the month, we shall have no option but to insist that you make immediate alternative arrangements—

She sheered her mind away, as she always did. Had to. Because to do anything else was unbearable.

I have to get the money! I have to!

It didn't matter how—it couldn't matter. She had to pay that bill—just *had* to!

Fear gnawed at her as she stared at the letter, at the stark, pitiless words in it.

As stark and pitiless as the world. She knew that now. The world was a vile place, without mercy or kindness or goodness in it. Hadn't she learnt that? Hadn't the last four punishing, terrifying years taught her that?

Into her eyes a hardness came, glazing them over. What use were feelings, sensibilities, moral revulsion? Where did they get you? Nowhere. The end of the road.

But for her the road stretched on. Endlessly. And, whatever

anyone thought of her, whatever she thought of herself, the money had to be found. *Had* to be!

In her head she heard the scornful, condemning words of Nikos Kazandros pouring over her, cruel and vicious, like acid into an unstanched wound.

'Take a good hard look at yourself when you get home—a good hard look, Sophie—and think about whether you like what you see. Ask yourself why you're doing what you're doing.'

Anger filled her. What did he know?

Well, *she* knew! She knew, all right! She could hate it all she liked, but nothing would let her off the hook—nothing could spare her.

Ahead of her another day loomed, another struggle.

And no end in sight.

And Nikos Kazandros, and all her memories of him, could take their sneers and contempt and drain away, back into the poisoned, bitter past where they belonged. And go to hell!

Nikos sat motionless in the leather chair at the head of an oval table around which half a dozen men were seated. They were discussing a forthcoming property deal, but Nikos wasn't paying attention. He had two people of his own in the discussion, whose judgement he trusted, and his presence was only as a figurehead for Kazandros Corp. Since his father had retired, two years previously, Nikos now had the entire running of the company to himself. After leaving London four years ago, he'd immersed himself without pause in learning every string there was to the business, cutting more and more deals on his own account until he'd earned his father's complete trust. He'd come a long way in four years….

And he'd never looked back. Not once. He had not permitted himself to do so. He had pushed Sophie Granton out of his head, never to return.

But return she had.

Damn her!

In the darkness of the night he'd been determined to push her back out of his head again. But this morning, with the bright sunshine streaming into the meeting room of his UK lawyers, she had come invading again.

He kept seeing her everywhere, all the time.

But not the way she'd been, draped on Cosmo Dimistris's arm. And not the way he'd known her four bitter years ago. Neither of those images burned in his skull.

It was the last image of her, when she'd sat hunched in the taxi, shivering, bedraggled, sodden.

Something moved in him—something he did not want to feel. He resented it. Why should he feel it? Sophie Granton was nothing to him! He knew what she was—what she was prepared to do to get what she wanted. If she'd got herself into a mess, it was none of his making! If she'd thought the world owed her an easy living and was now finding it did not, that was not his problem! It hadn't been four years ago, and it damn well wasn't now!

Deliberately, he pushed the image out of his head again. Pulled another one into its place. The one of her in the tarty evening gown, selling her company to Cosmo.

And who else…?

His eyes darkened suddenly. She'd got a scare last night, and he hadn't minced his words in laying it on the line for her just exactly what she was doing, but did that mean she was going to mend her ways? Or did she still think that she could get away with it? Getting men to pay for her company and nothing more?

And what if they didn't like her saying no to them…? What if next time she wasn't able to get out and get away? A man like Cosmo Dimistris wouldn't have any qualms about helping himself, and there were plenty of slimeballs in the world with the same views about women! She'd got lucky last night because Cosmo had simply helped himself to one of the other, more willing girls at the party. But another time she might not be so lucky. Another time she might find herself in serious danger….

Beneath his breath, an expletive formed. Damn the girl! Damn her!

Abruptly, he straightened in his seat. He got to his feet.

'Gentlemen, my apologies. Please conclude without me.' He nodded at his team, then turned and walked out of the room.

He needed to make a phone call.

'I'll just go and check if we have that in your size, madam,' Sophie said, keeping her voice rigorously polite, even though the woman she was serving had not thought it necessary to speak to her with even the minimum of courtesy. But difficult and demanding customers were something Sophie had had to learn how to handle, however obnoxious they were. Or however tired or dispirited she was.

Or desperate.

Because desperate was what she was. Eating like acid into her brain, the words of the letter kept going round and round in her head…

Unless the fees are paid in full…

She wanted to laugh hysterically. Scream. Dig her nails into her palms until they drew blood. Fighting down her panic, she found the shoe box and hefted it down. Then, surreptitiously looking around her, because the shop manageress was draconian about personal calls for staff, she slipped her mobile out of her pocket and checked for messages.

Yes! There was one! Fumblingly, she clicked it open and read, and as she did so her stomach plunged in a churning mix of emotions. It was another booking from the agency. The escort agency.

That's what it is—to me! I won't let it be anything else, I won't! It's just an escort agency....

She felt a spurt of anger. Nikos had mocked her for calling it an introduction service—but that was exactly what it called itself, she argued defensively. Its upmarket website proclaimed 'elite introductions for elite businessmen seeking elite companions'. She'd taken that at face value—but was she being pathetically naïve, blinding herself deliberately to what was beneath the respectable veneer? Well, it wouldn't be the first time she'd been fooled by a respectable-sounding organisation....

The familiar flush of shame and bitterness flared through her. Dear God, where did naïvety end and criminal stupidity begin?

The hollow inside her hardened, and she lifted her chin. Tough. *Tough.* No point whatsoever in repining the past and the appalling, criminally stupid mistakes she'd made! Because it was too late—she'd made them. And now she had to take the consequences. And the consequences were that she had no choice—no *choice* but to do what she was doing now.

Whatever it takes, however sordid the job, I have to do it. I have to make whatever money I can, however I can—I just have to.

And if that meant doing what was loathsome to her, if that meant reading this text message from the agency and being grateful—dear God, *grateful!*—for the fact that she was being booked again for tonight, then that was what she had to be. Inside her head, a nugget of fear reared its head. What if the man she was to meet tonight was just the same as Cosmo Dimistris? What if he thought he was booking a lot more than a companion for the evening? With an effort that cost her, she forced down the fear, the incipient panic. Well, she would just have to deal with it if it happened. Just as she'd had to deal with everything that had happened since her world had fallen apart....

'Your customer's getting shirty—better hurry up.'

The voice of one of the other sales assistants roused Sophie from her troubled thoughts. Hastily, she grabbed the requisite shoe box and hurried out. She could feel her stomach rumble, but ignored it. She never ate lunch any more, it was a waste of money. Every penny she could save went to a far, far better cause than herself. She never spent money on anything other than the barest minimum. She ate as little as possible, as cheaply as possible, endured a freezing cold bedsit to avoid heating costs, walked everywhere she possibly could.

As for clothes—apart from the repellent outfit she'd had to buy for her escort work, which she'd got in a charity shop anyway, she'd bought nothing for longer than she could remember.

For a moment—brief, poignant—a memory flashed in her head, vivid and piercing.

The evening dress I wore to the Covent Garden gala that first, magical night with Nikos! That beautiful, beautiful dress...

Her mouth thinned. Well, that was gone—along with every other designer dress she'd owned.

Along with everything else. Including the life she had once lived.

She swallowed. Sentiment was pointless. Worse than pointless. Unaffordable.

'You took your time!' The petulant tones of her customer penetrated.

'I'm so sorry…'

Forcing an apologetic smile to her lips, Sophie got on with her job.

Nikos sat at a table in the bar of the West End hotel, one he never frequented himself. His expression was grim. It had been ever since he'd phoned the escort agency Cosmo had booked Sophie through. Getting the number had meant an unpleasant phone conversation with Cosmo, who had not missed the opportunity both to complain about Sophie running out on him and to jibe at Nikos's sudden interest in girls of her kind.

But his expression had got even grimmer after he'd phoned the agency, and now, as he glanced at his watch impatiently, it was black. His eyes flicked to the hotel entrance again. She should be here any minute.

And then she was there, walking into the bar, her gait stiff, her posture tense. Nikos felt emotion kick in him, intense, hard.

It should have been anger. Anger that despite all his dire warnings to her about the true nature of what she was doing she had clearly ignored him. But, though anger was there, it was not the predominant emotion.

What emotion it was precisely he didn't know, didn't care. Knew only that it came with a leap in his veins that was like a tongue of scorching wind on a forest fire. Her presence instantly, immediately filled the space—filled his consciousness.

She was wearing the same outfit she'd worn the evening before, advertising her wares to the whole world. Yet she seemed oblivious to the fact. She was walking blindly, tautly, across the empty space from the hotel foyer into the bar. He watched her walking, waiting for the moment when she re-alised just who she was walking towards.

He saw when it happened. Saw her eyes widen abruptly, starkly, her face bleach, her stride falter. Saw the blankness in her face shatter like broken glass. As if she herself were shattering…

Then it was gone. The blankness was back. A rigid, frozen mask immobilising her face. He got up from his chair, con-fronting her. Her eyes darted sideways, searching past him. Nikos's mouth pulled into a caustic line. She was looking urgently for someone else. Anyone else. Just not him.

'Wrong call, Sophie,' he told her, and there was an edge in his voice like a blade. Her eyes whipped back to him, stared. Disbelieving. And somewhere deep in her eyes he saw something that he could not fail to recognise.

Panic. Dismay.

But beneath them was something else. Something that made the emotion slicing through him quicken, though he fought against it.

She was staring at him. The shock—disbelief—flaring in her eyes. No, this couldn't be. No. Not him. Not *him*. Not Nikos…

The denial was flighting through her, urgent, vehement. Oh, God, how could this be? How could it *be*? She fought for coherence, comprehension.

This can't be happening. It can't, it can't!

She couldn't be seeing Nikos again, not after it had taken all her strength to cope with what had happened the night before. How could she endure seeing him again? Denial screamed in her mind, but it was like a bird smashing itself against an iron cage. It was Nikos—there, waiting for her. Taunting her. Mocking her.

She summoned the only weapon she could, crushing down

every other emotion. Her face hardened. 'What's this farce all about, Nikos?' she demanded, every muscle in her body like steel under impossible tension. Her voice was as hard as her expression.

So was his. 'Sit down.' He pulled out a facing chair, holding it for her.

He saw her balking, and lifted one eyebrow sardonically. 'I said, sit down, Sophie. I've engaged your services this evening, so start earning your money.'

Sophie sat, her legs suddenly soggy. Numbly, she watched Nikos fold his long, lean body, clad in a superb hand-made suit, into the opposite chair, every centimetre of him assured, sleek, powerful.

Devastating.

She felt the hollow gape in her stomach, felt emotions rush into the space, churning and convulsing. Overpowering.

Nikos, so close she could see every line and plane of his face! So close she could reach out and touch him!

No! Desperately she fought against the rush of blood as her gaze clung to the man opposite her. No! That was all— the only word she must keep in her head. No! No to everything that made her want to go to him, that made the pulse quicken in her veins, the breath tighten in her lungs.

She opened her mouth to speak, to voice her protest at what was happening, but he was there before her.

'I've booked you for tonight, Sophie, for one reason and one reason only,' he said, and his voice was steely.

His face was shuttered, jaw set. His eyes bored into her, pinioning her. She could not move, could only endure— frozen, immobile.

'Didn't I tell you last night what a dangerous game you were playing?' he iced out. 'You're standing at the gutter's edge, Sophie, and it will take only a single step to be in it! You can think yourself unsullied because you call it escorting, but that's not what others will think, believe me!'

His hard eyes excoriated her. 'I thought I'd got the message home to you last night, but I haven't, have I? You're still on the agency's books, and your presence here right now is proof you haven't wised up yet. Or won't!' He took a sharp intake of breath. 'You got lucky last night, Sophie! That jerk Cosmo had other girls to help himself to, so he didn't turn nasty on you! That won't happen every time! And a man like that, who thinks he's paying for a woman for the night, won't take kindly to being told, sorry, but you'll go home to your virtuous single bed at midnight!'

Her face was closed, shutting him out, rejecting what he was saying. 'I can handle myself,' she retorted, quelling the churning inside her. She wanted to leap to her feet, run, but she couldn't move, could hardly get words out while he laid into her.

'Like hell!' he shot back dismissively. 'Last night you saw the kind of scene that the men who'll hire you like to enjoy! All it will take is a spiked drink, or worse, and a little exercise of masculine strength. And you don't think anyone at a place like that is going to believe your protests, do you? Do you *want* to end up drugged and raped?'

Her face was white under the make-up. 'It won't happen! I'll be careful! I'll stick to public places, like this.'

Nikos's voice was scathing. 'And then what, Sophie? Have you thought that through? Because I have, believe me! And it's the reason you're sitting here right now. Let me spell it out for you.' He took another scissored breath. 'You may not give a cent for your reputation, you may not care if the whole world knows your line of work, but spare a thought, if you please—' his voice was edged with scathing sarcasm '—for others. Whether you get into serious trouble with a demanding client or not, you'll cause trouble for others. Think of your father, Sophie. Whatever his business problems, he wasn't responsible for the way you behaved four years ago. His fault was in indulging you, making you think you could have everything you wanted, the easy way. But he wouldn't want this for you now, what you're doing—what father would?'

A steel band had started to tighten around her skull, digging into her skin. 'He won't know.' It was all she could get out and it cost her, even to say that.

Nikos's eyes hardened. 'You think? By swanning around in public places people will see you—people who know you. After all…' he paused '…I did.' He paused again, his eyes boring into her like drills. 'And I won't be the only one to make the conclusion I did about you last night. Do you think anyone is actually going to *believe* your claim that you only sell your company—not your body?' His voice was harsh, pitiless. 'They'll call you a hooker, a whore, a call-girl— whether you like it or not!'

The unbearable lecture went on, and she wanted to scream and yell, but she couldn't—she couldn't. She had to sit there and take it, endure it.

'And then, Sophie, what about when the tabloids cotton on to what you're doing? Someone will spot you and tip them off. And it doesn't matter that Granton plc is no more, they'll dredge it back up and they'll have a field day exposing how a millionaire's daughter has ended up on the game now Daddy's run out of his millions. They'll revel in it, Sophie! You can protest your innocence all you like, but they'll still put "escort agency" in quotes, and everyone will know it's just a euphemism, whether you like it or not. Then some kindly soul will put the tabloid rag in front of your father, with a sympathetic look on their face, and your father will know just how far his precious darling daughter has fallen….'

The band was red-hot now—red-hot against her forehead. If only he would stop, just *stop*…

She could feel her nails almost piercing her palms, feel the pain spiking up her arms. And still he went on, hectoring and lecturing.

'It's a sleazy, sordid world you're moving in, and you can give it all the prettied-up anodyne names you like, dress it up however you please, but that doesn't hide the truth of it! So face up to it.'

She wanted to laugh—harsh, bitter—in his damn face. *Face up to it?* Dear God, wasn't that what she was doing? What she had no choice but to do? Facing up to the fact that she had to find money—any amount, by any means—because to fail…to fail…

No—failure wasn't an option. She had to find the money. And if that meant looking at herself in the mirror and hating what she saw, being repulsed by what she saw, then so be it She could not afford pride, self-respect or self-loathing to get in her way.

She took a cold, icy breath, freezing her lungs, her voice. 'Don't lecture me, Nikos! I told you, I am not doing this from *choice*! I need the money!'

'How much?'

She stared.

He gave a rasp of irritation. 'I said, how much?'

Her chin lifted. 'What's it to you?'

Anger, controlled but visible, flashed in his eyes. 'Just answer me.'

He wanted to know? She told him, nails digging into her palms. 'Five thousand pounds.'

That was what she had to have—enough to see her clear, at least for the next couple of months. After that—well, time enough to worry then…

As it always did when she had to think about the endless requirement for money, her mind cut out. To do anything else was far, far too frightening.

'Five thousand?' Nikos echoed the amount in a harsh voice. 'And you think you can clear that kind of money just by working as a no-sex escort? A little light evening work, just smiling and chatting and looking sexy?' He didn't bother to hide his sarcasm. 'Why do you need the money, anyway?'

Her nails dug deeper. Tension netted around her. 'I owe it.'

'Paying off credit cards that have stopped funding you, is that it? So why not just go to Daddy and get him to bail you out—or has he finally stopped indulging you?'

The band around her head was tightening more. 'He doesn't know I owe the money.' She spoke tersely. It was all she could manage.

Nikos looked at her. So she was hiding not just her life-style from her father but her debts, as well. For a moment he considered tracking down Edward Granton and putting him in the picture. Then he disposed of the thought. The man did not deserve to know the unsavoury truth about his daughter now, much as he hadn't needed to know what she had tried four years ago. However, Sophie had to be stopped, right now, from the course she was so rashly taking. Time to cut to the chase. It galled him to do it, but it was necessary—that was all.

'Very well. I will settle your debts for you. I will give you the five thousand pounds.'

She heard the words, heard them but could not take them in. He was offering her the money she so desperately needed?

For a moment emotion knifed in her like a sword. Then a word formed on her lips.

'Why?'

'Because, Sophie, it's in my interests.'

Emotion knifed again. She wanted to lash out at him, tell him he could take his money and go to hell! She would never, never take a penny from him! Never!

His eyes were like steel hooks, holding hers. 'Once the tabloids pick up on you, they will dig into your background—and what will they find, Sophie? *Who* will they find?' His voice was edged, like a razorblade. 'They'll find me. They'll find that I once—*dated*—you.' He said the word as if it were poison. 'And then they'll drag me into the mud that you're wading into. The Greek tabloids will pick up the story, linking a Kazandros to a hooker—because that's what they'll call you, however coyly—and then my parents will hear of it. I won't have that, Sophie. I really won't.' His voice was hard, icy. 'So I'm prepared to hand over the five thousand pounds you say you owe. But—' he held up a peremptory hand '—not only do you ditch the escort agency and never go near it again, you also clear out of London.'

Her answer was automatic. 'I can't. I can't leave London.'

'You want my money—you leave London.'

'I live here.' She kept her answers short. It was all she could manage.

She saw him give a shrug. 'You can come back. But not till Cosmo Dimistris is out of the country, you've rusticated long enough, and I'm out of the UK, as well.'

Her emotions were churning. Aggression, resentment, and so much more—all in a concrete mixer, heaving around inside her. Mixing with the voice inside her.

Don't listen to him! You can't take his money—you can't!

But hope, desperation, seared like hot steel through her brain.

Oh, God, he could hand me the money. It means nothing to him, just loose change, but to me…to me…

She tried to cut her mind off. Tried not to let the words form in her head, the pleading, the hope, flaring like a thin, impossible flame.

I can't! I can't take his money! It's impossible! Impossible! Anyone but him…anyone! Not him—not him!

Not Nikos Kazandros. Not the man who had once been everything to her. A dream come true, a dream of bliss— until the dream had turned into a nightmare. A nightmare that had never left her. A nightmare she had to cope with day in, day out. That and the desperate need for money— so desperate that she'd been prepared to take on the vile work that Nikos was lecturing her about. Standing at the gutter's edge, the way he'd said. And if she was prepared to do that, then why be squeamish about taking money from Nikos?

It's money—that's all that matters. Money you need, money you've got to have—because if you don't have it then you know what's going to happen. And who cares where it comes from? You were ready enough to earn it by draping yourself over any man who paid you! So who the hell do you think you are to be so damn delicate now, saying you can't touch Nikos Kazandros's money because he once ripped every stupid, pathetic illusion from you!

The voice stabbed brutally at her, merciless and harsh, telling her what she didn't want to know, didn't want to face. But she had to face it. Had learnt in the bitter years since her world had crashed around her that running away was not an option. That facing the brutal realities of life, of the life that she had been plunged into, forced into, was all she could do.

Her lesson had been hard. Bitterly hard.

But she had learnt it.

Her lips pressed together tightly; her hands clenched. If Nikos Kazandros was offering her five thousand pounds she would take it. Grab it. Seize it. What did her pride matter? Her heart? Her feelings?

They had stopped mattering four years ago, when everything had crashed around her.

Her eyes were like stone, her voice short and sharp as she addressed him. 'How long will that be?' she demanded aggressively.

'How long?' He echoed her demand. 'A couple of weeks? Then you can do what the hell you want.'

Sophie's mind raced. Homing in on the essentials.

'I need the money before then.' She spoke tersely, grittily.

'You can have a cheque when you're out of London.'

She had seen his eyes flash, flare with brief anger at the way she was speaking to him. She didn't care.

'Where do I have to go? I can't leave the country.' She spelt that out up-front. She could be out of London for two weeks, just about, but she couldn't be out of the country. She needed to know she was only a train ride from London, not risk being stranded abroad, unable to afford the fare home.

Nikos's mouth thinned. 'Don't worry, Sophie, I'm not whisking you off to some romantic hideaway.' The sarcasm bit at her, but she ignored that too. She would ignore everything about Nikos Kazandros—everything except the money he was offering her. The lifeline…

Emotion stabbed inside her again, despite her attempt to crush it back. Dear God—money and Nikos Kazandros…

Nikos Kazandros, offering a lifeline…

The lifeline he had refused to offer before.

The irony of it twisted in her consciousness.

But the lifeline I wanted then wasn't a paltry five thousand pounds...

No. The thought seared like a burning brand in her head. It was a lot more. Far, far more than money...

She sheered her mind away. No point treading that bitter path again. The path paved with broken dreams. She made herself meet his gaze, made herself look at those dark, cold eyes. Eyes that had once melted her in their heat.

But never would again.

For a second, a fraction of a second so brief she hardly registered it, she felt emotion so powerful, so agonising, that she felt faint with it. Then it was gone. Only the expressionless, indifferent gaze on her was left.

'So where—?' she began, her voice demanding again.

This time he cut her short. He got to his feet. 'I'll send a car,' he told her. 'Be ready at eight tomorrow morning.'

'That's too early,' she said immediately. It would give her no time to go into the shop, explain what was happening, hope they would let her disappear for two weeks without sacking her. But even if they did sack her, she would have to accept it and then just try and get another job swiftly when she was allowed back to London again.

'Tough.' His reply was unsympathetic.

She glared at him, but said nothing. She had no choice but to take what was handed out to her. Just the way she had for four hideous years. Taking everything thrown at her. Swallowing it. Enduring it.

And she would endure this too. Because the lifeline he was tossing at her was one she could not afford to throw back in his face.

He waited, pointedly, as she moved around the table.

'I'll have my driver take you home now,' he told her, pulling out his mobile to summon his car. 'Give you time to pack.'

She said nothing. She couldn't think, couldn't do anything except let him steer her out of the hotel on to the pavement. A sleek saloon was there already, and the driver got out, opening the rear passenger door for her. How many times had she shared Nikos's chauffeured car, been out with him in the evening? Been escorted home by him, her heart singing with bliss…?

She pulled her gaze away. Away from his tall, commanding figure that could make her heart skip a beat just looking at it.

But not any more.

Never again.

As she plunged inside the car, scooping her long, clinging skirt out of the way as she did so, she twisted her head away, staring out of the far window at the traffic coursing heedlessly by. Refusing to look back at Nikos.

The driver spoke to her on his intercom, and she gave him her address then hunkered further back into the corner of her seat, still not looking out at Nikos, not knowing if he were even still there or not as the car pulled out into the traffic.

On the pavement, heedless of passers-by, Nikos stood stock still, staring after the disappearing car. His face was expressionless. But inside, virulently, he was calling himself every kind of fool for having allowed himself to see her again, to do this face to face instead of setting one of his staff to sort it, keeping himself well away from her. Too late now, though—it was done. Sophie was dealt with, and also the danger she threatened his family with. Silencing his castigations, he reached out his hand to flag down a passing taxi.

Heading the other way.

The way that did not have Sophie Granton in its path.

CHAPTER FIVE

NIKOS gazed abstractedly out across the expanse of his London office, filled with late morning light, and wondered what Sophie Granton was making of her new accommodation. It would be quite a shock for her, that was for certain. He gave a thin, humourless smile. A luxury venue it was not.

What had she been expecting? he wondered to himself. That he would keep her in the comfort she was so used to? His smile narrowed to a tight, whipped line. After all, that had always been his main purpose in her life, as far as she was concerned...

That was what he must make himself remember about Sophie Granton. Nothing else.

Nothing about the way she'd used to smile at him, the way they would talk, endlessly, about anything and everything. The way she'd gaze at him, her eyes sparkling like diamonds, when he complimented her. Or the way they'd laughed together, danced together, walked hand in hand together...

He snapped his mind away. What the hell was the point in thinking back to a past he never wanted to remember again? What, indeed, was the point of thinking about Sophie Granton at all?

None, he told himself resolutely. He had done what was

necessary to minimise the risk to his family from her sordid lifestyle and that was enough. Anything else was irrelevant.

Irrelevant to think about her now, to think about where she was now, wondering what she was doing, what she made of where he had stashed her to keep her away from London, from Cosmo—from himself.

Because that was why he'd sent her out of town, he knew. To keep her far, far away from him.

Far away was the safest place for Sophie Granton to be.

So he would be safe from her and all that she had once meant to him—and never could again.

With a short, sharp, decisive intake of breath, he reached for his keyboard and got on with his work.

Hot sunlight was baking down, and Sophie could feel sweat trickling down into the small of her back beneath her already damp T-shirt. She rolled her shoulders a moment, stretching her neck, the movement shifting the crouching position she was in and making her rebalance her muscles as she lifted her gaze. A brief, wry expression formed in her eyes as a glance reaffirmed her surroundings.

Was it really only four days since she had been deposited here? It seemed a lot longer. A lot longer since she had climbed, tensely, into the sleek chauffeured car that had been parked so incongruously at the kerb of the bleak, blighted street where she had to live now. Her stomach had been tied into knots, and the mental hardness she'd relied on the previous night to get through the ordeal of seeing Nikos again had dissolved into a morass of viscous, glutinous, conflicting emotions that she'd scarcely been able to give a name to.

One thing she'd known for certain. Reaction had set in with a vengeance. As she'd lain sleepless, stomach churning, in her narrow, lumpy bed, trying not to hear the thump of music coming through the thin walls from the next bedsit, she had realised that the only thing that had got her through the shock of seeing Nikos again had been nothing more than bravado.

How did I even manage to face him? How did I stop myself bolting the moment I laid eyes on him in that hotel bar?

It was what she should have done, she knew. And yet it had happened so fast, so out of the blue, when her nerves had already been at stretching point, and she had been unable to act rationally.

And then, even more out of the blue, for him actually to dangle that lifeline over her…

Five thousand pounds—just to stay out of London for two weeks!

She had known she shouldn't take the money. Shouldn't touch it. But it had been impossible not to. Impossible not to grab at it with both hands, to snatch it, even from a man who should have been the very last man to be indebted to.

But when the car's driver had handed her an envelope with her name on it, and she had seen the cheque within, her last resolve had evaporated. The numbers had danced in front of her eyes and she had felt a relief so profound go through her that it had made her realise just how frightened she had been about the punishing need to get hold of the money somehow, anyhow…

It hadn't been until the driver had stopped, at her request, at a branch of her bank, and she'd raced in to deposit the cheque, simultaneously writing out one of her own with an accompanying note and then posting it in the nearest postbox, that she had felt herself truly believe in the reprieve that she had had. But back in the car she had felt her anxiety levels start to mount again.

Nothing came free in life—she knew that know, knew it

bitterly and harshly. So what was Nikos going to expect of her in repayment for the loan? Just where, exactly, was she to be taken?

Now, as the sun's heat burned down on her, Sophie's wry expression deepened. Of all the possible destinations she'd guessed Nikos had had in mind for her as a way of keeping her out of London for a fortnight, this had never been one of them. This was a world away from anything she had envisaged.

Four days ago the car had deposited her here. Just where 'here' was, she still did not exactly know! But she didn't care. It was enough just to be there. Somewhere heading west out of London, in the depths of the English countryside, in what she could only assume was one of Kazandros Corp's latest UK property acquisitions.

A beautiful but semi-derelict, utterly deserted country house.

Not that she was in the main house itself. The small wing she was inhabiting had clearly once been something like the quarters for a housekeeper, or thereabouts, judging by the modest and old-fashioned décor and furnishings, the small rooms and out-of-the-way position. Just how long ago a housekeeper had inhabited these quarters Sophie could not tell, except that it was not recently.

Her first task had been to give the place a thorough clean, removing layers of dust and neglect. She had welcomed the work, though, finding pleasure in the effort required not least because it gave her something to do. It was the same in the small walled garden that she was now so diligently weeding. The place was a sun-trap, and Sophie needed nothing more to wear than a T-shirt and cotton trousers as the summer's heat baked down on her in the enclosed space.

It had taken her a while to realise that she had the entire place to herself. Not only had there been no one in evidence when she had arrived, no one had put in an appearance since. For a while she'd wondered at it, then simply accepted it. She had not been completely abandoned, however, for she had discovered upon her arrival that the fridge in the old-fashioned kitchen was working, and had been filled with food—basic, but adequate for about a week. The larder had an equally adequate complement of groceries. She had initially wondered if someone was going to turn up the next day, but no one did, nor had since. Nor was there any sign of life in the main house.

She had explored that the afternoon of her arrival, and as she'd wandered through the huge, deserted, dusty rooms, with their shutters closed, and bereft of furniture and hangings, she had been struck both by the melancholy of the place and its striking beauty. Restored, the house would be breathtakingly beautiful! Even as she'd gazed around, though, she'd known it would take a fortune to restore it. Floorboards were sagging, moulding was coming off the ceilings, and there was a smell of mildew everywhere. Cobwebs festooned the cornices, and she could hear the tell-tale scuttlings of mice in the wainscoting. She had not dared venture upstairs, for the graceful curving banisters were precarious, and who knew how rotten the floorboards might be? It was not a place to explore on her own.

What was Nikos intending to do with the place? she'd wondered. Turn it into another prestige country hotel? A conference centre or other business use? Or restore it and sell it as residence for a millionaire? Her eyes had worked around the elegant proportions of the rooms, mentally envisaging it restored as a private house once more.

How beautiful to live here!

Out of nowhere, like a poisoned dart, the thought had struck her.

We could have lived here—Nikos and I...

Instantly she'd scourged the words from her mind, but it had been too late. Imagination, vivid and painful, had flared through her.

Nikos and me—living here—in my dream of bliss and happy ever after...

For brief, piercing moments she had been able to see it, so real, so *real*!

What if my dream had come true? What if now, four years later, we were here, together?

She had felt the ache in her heart. Four years had not diminished one iota Nikos's impact on her! He must be thirty-two now, and his blazing masculinity had only matured. In her mind's eye she saw his imprint—the familiar twist of his beautiful mouth, the achingly lush sweep of his eyelashes, the drowning darkness of his eyes. Nothing had been lost from all that she had been so fascinated by! He was still the most devastating man she had ever set eyes on—could ever set eyes on—setting her pulse beating like a bird in flight....

Danger had flickered like a hot flame.

Making her start back.

No! To think of Nikos again was madness—and to let herself imagine herself here with him nothing less than insanity!

Furiously, she had roused herself from her memory and opened at random another pair of double doors, hating herself for having allowed such thoughts entrance to her head. But the moment she'd stepped into the next room she had wished she had not. Her eyes had gone instantly to the grand piano in the centre of the room. Without conscious volition, she had found herself walking towards it, lifting up the heavy, dusty folds of the cover. The dark, gleaming wood beneath had brought a stab to her chest. How long had it been since she had last played? Abruptly she had dropped the cover, stepped back and turned on her heel out of the room, refusing to look back at the instrument.

She didn't like to see pianos any more. They only rammed home to her the total ruination of her life—a life she had once taken utterly for granted.

That was now gone for ever.

Angrily, she had marched back through the padded baize door into the servants' quarters, which led, meanderingly, to the housekeeper's wing. Her anger had been directed at herself, for having even for the briefest moment entertained such pointless, fatuous fantasy.

Her and Nikos, living happily ever after…

The sharpened blade had slid into her all over again, and she'd wrenched it out viciously. Oh, God, why, *why* had he walked back into her life? Hadn't she enough to cope with without this fresh torment?

Blindly, she had plunged out into the little walled garden, and now, after four days, she had made it her sole focus.

Her refuge.

It had drawn her from the moment she'd arrived. An old-fashioned walled kitchen garden, long smothered by weeds.

What had made her so determined to clear away what she could she didn't know—only that the mindless, repetitive work gave her occupation and brought her solace. Armed with some rusting tools she'd found in an outhouse, she'd set to, ripping out weeds and digging through the packed earth. Already she had found hidden treasures—a bed of ripening strawberries which, once cleared of choking weeks, was yielding ruby fruits day on day.

The hours passed soothingly. Hot and sunny in the sheltered domain, with the scents of summer all around her, the vegetation verdant and lush. The quietness was interrupted only by birdsong, the somnolent buzz of bees and insects, and the air wafted by the breeze soughing in the trees beyond the walls. Sophie considered that an aching back and broken fingernails were a small price to pay for what she was getting in return—a blessed break from the grinding, bleak drudgery of her existence. A blessed break, too, even if only short-lived, from the constant anxiety and dread that now consumed her life.

Only one thing flawed her peace—an image she could not expunge from her mind. An image that burned with fresh pain, fresh bitterness, and that was as vivid, as indelible as it had ever been throughout the last four punishing, nightmare years: Nikos Kazandros, who had once been her foolish, puerile fantasy of happy ever after, and who was now only her torment.

Vehemently, she attacked the obdurate, deep-rooted weeds running riot in the soil as if she were digging out a far, far more invasive intruder into her memory, her thoughts…her very being.

All the way down the motorway, as the low-slung, powerful car cruised through the miles at a constant high speed, overtaking everything else on the road, Nikos knew he was in two minds. Two minds that weren't going to come together. Could never come together.

One mind told him very, very clearly that he really, adamantly, *definitely* shouldn't be doing this.

The other mind told him that there was nothing untoward whatsoever in doing it. It was a simple, rational, ordinary decision. Nothing to have doubts about.

After all, why should it be? His secretary had informed him that the particular historical architectural consultant he wanted, one of the country's leading experts on the period in question, would at short notice, owing to a cancellation, be able to meet him and go over the property with him. There was no absolute necessity for him to meet the man—he could, if he wished, simply hand the project over to one of his managers. But still, the architect in question was prestigious—knighted by the Queen, no less—and a recognised expert whose priority was restoration, not profit. Nikos did not want to come across as nothing more than a foreign businessman to whom the commercial aspects of the acquisition took precedence over the imperative of cultural preservation. Besides, no commercial gain could be realised if the restoration was not carried out perfectly, and by using this particular expert it would lend considerable cachet to the enterprise as a whole.

So Nikos's foot pressed down on the accelerator, and the powerful car scythed forward. It made sound, hard-headed business sense to meet the man today and expedite the restoration project thereby. And hard-headed business decisions were what Nikos always made. Unswayed by any other considerations.

His mouth tightened. There had been one time and one time only when he had nearly broken that rule.

He never had since.

Which was why he could right now afford to ignore the nagging that was going on in the other half of his mind. The one that said that he should have postponed this trip for a fortnight, that the last thing he should be doing was going within a hundred miles of the place.

Another thought flickered in his mind. He should have brought one of his managers with him. That would have been sensible. He'd need to appoint someone to oversee the project and report progress to him, so he really should have made a selection from his London team and driven down with him now.

A shrug moved his powerful shoulders. Well, he hadn't. That was all. He was meeting the architect on his own, and that was that. The project manager he appointed could make his own contact with the architect's consultancy office and take over from there. There was no need for him to be at this initial meeting.

Silencing the nagging, he went on driving.

Sophie leaned back on her heels and surveyed her handiwork. It really was encouraging how much better the garden looked now, after four solid days of clearing and digging. Pointless it might be, if no one continued her work and it went to weeds again, but at least it was within the scope of a single person to tackle it.

The place had become her haven. She welcomed the solitude, the absence of anyone else, and if it had been a little unnerving the first night to be so alone she had swiftly got used to it, welcoming the nocturnal silence punctuated only by the hooting of owls and the occasional bark of a fox. During the days no one came, and she relished the uninterrupted peace and quiet.

Stretching her muscles, she picked up the trowel again.

And stilled.

A car engine. A low, throaty note. Clearly approaching the house along the front drive. For a second she froze, then made herself stand up, ear cocked. She heard the car come to a halt and the engine cut out. There was a pause, then the slam of a door. Then nothing again.

She went on standing motionless, trowel in one hand, listening for any more evidence of who had just driven up.

A bad feeling started to go through her. She knew the kind of car that made that kind of throaty engine noise. Knew the kind of man who drove them. Had been driven by one herself in another life, a life long turned to ashes.

She wondered what to do. Retreat inside? Shut the doors and windows? Pretend she wasn't in? Almost she gave a nervous laugh, then stifled it. Oh, what the hell did she care if Nikos turned up here? What was it to her? Nothing—nothing at all! Just as she was nothing to him. Nothing. Ever again.

She dropped down to her heels and started attacking the nettles again, viciously jabbing at the soil around them so she could root them out. Root them out without them stinging her. Just as she had had to root out Nikos from her life—her heart. Her memory.

But digging him out had stung her mortally.

Nikos stared tight-lipped around him. There was no sign whatsoever of the damn architect! Irritably he glanced at his watch. It was dead on the hour of the appointment. He was never late for appointments—his time was too valuable for that. His mouth tightened even more. But that was apparently not a view shared by this prestigious historic house expert! Well, he would give the man five minutes, no more, then phone his PA and get her to find out what the hell was going on. In the meantime he might as well take another look at the place.

He had authorised its acquisition in the new year, and had visited it once, in February. Nikos had got the impression then of a house on the edge of serious ruin—one that had not, by any means, looked its best on that damp, bleak winter's day. But now...

He gazed around, an approving expression forming on his face. Yes, it had been a shrewd acquisition. The place needed massive restoration, but once completed its value would be beyond debate—a prestigious addition to his portfolio.

He started to walk along the frontage of the façade, glancing up and around, seeing in his mind's eye the perfected restoration of its classical proportions. But even as he did so he was conscious of a mental distraction.

Nothing to do with the tardy architect.

Everything to do with the temporary house guest inhabiting the former housekeeper's quarters.

His expression morphed. No longer approving, it became harder, harsher, with a cynical twist to his mouth now.

So how was the pampered profligate faring? She must be climbing the walls with boredom by now, repulsed by the humble surroundings she was being forced to live in. She who had always stepped so daintily through life, cushioned by her father's wealth and his pampering devotion, taking it all for granted, never worrying her beautiful blond head about the necessities of life. Drifting through it gracefully, artistically, carefree and lovely.

Memory, sliding like a stiletto into the soft, vulnerable tissues of his mind, came to him. Her face uplifted, so beautiful, her expression so tender, her pale long hair like a waterfall down her slender back.

He forced it aside. Conjured instead the memory of how she'd looked that evening in the hotel bar, in her tawdry glamour, designed to allure in the cheapest way. Yes, that was what he must remember. *All* that he must remember. That and the ugly truth that had lain beneath the surface of the girl he had once known, who had once meant so much to him. The truth that she had so recklessly revealed to him just in the very nick of time, before he had done something fatally stupid…

Restlessly, he turned the corner of the house and strode along the crunching, weed-infested terrace, bathed in sunshine that highlighted the broken flags and lichened balustrade. A long, stone wall, two metres high and more, curved away at the far end of the terrace, shielding the rear portions of the house where functional quarters had once been inhabited by the several dozen staff it would have taken to keep a property like this in pristine condition. Inset along the wall was a studded gate. He headed towards it, half curious as to what lay beyond, half glancing at his watch to see whether he should phone his PA yet.

The door was heavy, and grating, and did not open easily. But he shouldered it with a forcible push and it yielded. Beyond was what must once have been a kitchen garden, now completely run to weeds. A further wall bounded it on the far side, and he headed towards that too. Another studded door to shoulder open. Again he stepped through.

And stopped dead.

It was Sophie. He saw her instantly. Sophie kneeling on a brick pathway, her back to him. Even as he recognised her she twisted round jerkily, having heard the doorway forced open.

She froze. For a second Nikos neither moved nor spoke.

Then, abruptly, she scrambled to her feet.

Emotion shot through Nikos. A jumble, a tangle. Inconsistent and confused.

Sophie. Sophie so utterly, totally and completely *not* the way his last image of her was. Sophie a million miles away from the tawdry vamp in her cheap, tarty finery, face plastered in make-up, eyes like black holes, lashes clotted with mascara, mouth a scarlet slash. This Sophie could not have been more different. She was wearing some kind of faded cotton trousers, he dimly registered, with an equally faded T-shirt, and her hair was pulled up high on her head in a ponytail, then twisted round loosely into a straggling knot. Her face was completely bare of make-up—unless the streak of what looked like dried earth across one cheekbone could class as such. Another smear of dried earth was on the thigh of her right trouser leg, and there was a snaggle of goosegrass caught on her shoulder. Her right hand was clutching a trowel as if for dear life.

He stepped towards her, a frown creasing his brow at the total change in her. Automatically she took a step backwards. The movement irritated him—annoyed him. Made him speak more sharply than he'd meant.

'What do you think you're doing?'

She flinched. He could see it. But her chin went up. Two flags of colour flared across her cheeks, as though some emotion were running in her.

'Gardening,' she answered shortly. Then, even more shortly, 'I'm sorry if I'm not supposed to—'

He frowned, but not at the tone of her voice. 'Why are you doing it?' This was not what he had in a million years thought he would find her doing.

'It's something to do,' she said. Her voice was still abrupt, her mind still desperately trying to get some degree of control back. She felt as if she'd just been knocked for six, looking up to see Nikos striding up to her out of nowhere. 'And it obviously needs doing,' she heard herself going on. 'This place is going to rack and ruin.'

Her words jogged Nikos's recollection that he was waiting for the damn architect to show up. Impatiently, he yanked out his mobile and phoned his PA.

Taking hasty advantage of his preoccupation, Sophie bolted indoors, cheeks still burning, heart pounding suddenly. Oh, God, *why* had Nikos turned up? How could she cope with him being here? She plunged into the kitchen and started vigorously washing her soil-smeared hands, as if she could wash Nikos down the plughole at he same time. Her heart was still hammering away, and she could feel panic rising in her. With harsh, deep breaths, she fought for control.

Outside, Nikos registered that she'd raced away even as his PA picked up the phone. A moment later and his annoyance had deepened. The architect had been delayed, and wanted the appointment rearranged for the following day. Angrily agreeing, he hung up and slipped the phone back into his jacket pocket. The gesture suddenly made him aware of how hot he was.

He strode indoors, finding himself in a poky living room, giving way to an equally poky kitchen beyond, where he could hear the sound of a tap running. He ducked his head beneath the low lintel and went in. The coolness of the interior was a relief, the thick walls keeping the heat out. At the kitchen sink Sophie was scrubbing her hands.

'Is that drinking water?' he asked, his voice still abrupt, both from his annoyance with the architect and from seeing Sophie again. Why the latter should be disturbing him only annoyed him more.

She snapped her head round, as if she had not expected him to be there.

'Yes,' she answered. She didn't want him coming near her, so she seized an up ended glass from the draining board, filled it up, and placed it on the kitchen table, averting her gaze deliberately.

Murmuring a brief thanks, Nikos drank the contents down in one. The water was chill, and tasted good. Reviving. He glanced about him. Sophie was scrubbing her nails with a nailbrush, vigorously and busily. He watched her go on doing it for some moments. Finally, as if she could occupy herself no longer, she turned off the tap, seized a dishtowel, and dried her hands—just as vigorously and busily. Then she turned and faced Nikos. She couldn't go on staring at the kitchen wall for ever.

Instead, she found herself staring at something much more disastrous.

Nikos. Nikos a few feet from her. Nikos looking a million dollars in one of his hand-made suits, moulding his tall, lean body, tailored to perfection, just as the body beneath was honed to perfection. Just as his incredible face was. Perfection.

Unlike her. She was cruelly, humiliatingly aware of what she looked like—dirty and sweaty and caught totally unawares. Well, she wouldn't feel that way—why should she? Why should she care what Nikos thought of her ever again?

And yet there was something she did have to say to him. She was burningly conscious of it. She didn't want to, but she knew she had to. Even so, it came out gratingly.

'Thank you for lending me the money. I'll pay it back as soon as I can, but I can't do it quickly—I'm sorry.'

Did surprise flicker in those night-dark eyes? She didn't know. Didn't want to look. Nor did it matter, after all—just as nothing about his reaction to her mattered.

He gave a shrug of his broad, elegantly clothed shoulders.

'It's not important. Getting you away from London, away from the gutter's edge, was important.'

Sophie felt her jaw tighten. 'I'll pay it back,' she persisted. How she had no idea. Nor when. But pay it back she would—if it took her years! She would not be beholden to Nikos Kazandros!

He gave another dismissive shrug and she felt anger bite in her. He couldn't have made it clearer that he couldn't care less about losing five thousand pounds! It was chickenfeed to him. To her it was—salvation.

Then he was speaking again. 'If you want to do me a favour, you could make me something to eat—I skipped lunch getting here.'

She stiffened. She didn't want him hanging around here— she wanted him gone. Whatever reason he'd come here for, she just wanted him out!

'It's not exactly your standard of cuisine,' she retorted.

A dark, saturnine eyebrow lifted in response. 'Nor yours, either, is it, Sophie? You're used to more luxury than this.'

There was a jibe in his voice. She could hear it distinctly. She swallowed down a retort. What was the point of spitting back? But her silence must have irritated him. The glint in his eye told her that.

'This isn't what you were expecting, is it?' he posed. 'Did you think I was going to put you up in the lap of luxury for a fortnight's easy living?'

'It doesn't matter what I thought, does it?' she made herself reply evenly. She would not rise to him, however much he needled her. 'And anyway, this place is very peaceful.'

Nikos's expression changed. Peaceful? What kind of an-swer was that? And yet he realised it was true. Though humble, these surroundings *were* peaceful. Was that what Sophie Granton liked these days? His eyes went to her again—registering with another start of bemusement how totally different she looked.

At home here.

Well, if she had made herself at home, she could make him a meal! He was definitely growling with hunger. 'So—do I get a late lunch? A sandwich will do.' His tone changed. So did the expression in his eyes. 'You've fixed me a sandwich before now—remember?'

Remember?

Oh, yes, she remembered, all right...

Instantly Sophie's vision cut her back in time.

CHAPTER SIX

MIDNIGHT—they'd been to the theatre, eaten beforehand, then afterwards wandered along the South Bank, holding hands, counting the dolphins carved curlingly around the Victorian lampposts, talking of nothing and everything, until her feet in her high heels had ached. Nikos had conjured a car from nowhere and taken her home, and they'd realised how hungry they were. So she'd taken him down to the kitchen and made him a towering club sandwich with half the contents of the fridge. It had toppled over on the table and they had burst out laughing, and he'd caught her, and kissed her, and kissed her again...and she'd been dazed and dizzy with bliss...

Pain, like a knife, sliced through her memory, cutting it away. Deliberately she purged it.

'It will only be cheese and ham,' she warned, her voice terse. She didn't want to make him a sandwich. Didn't want him standing there, so damnably close. Didn't want him anywhere near her. Disturbing her. Making her feel his overwhelming presence in the close, confining space.

Why does he have this impact on me? How? I'm not twenty any more, and I'm way, way past caring about men—but this one...

This one still overwhelmed her. This one still had the same power he'd always had! Four years had done nothing to change that.

Quiveringly aware of him, she yanked open the fridge door. At least making him a sandwich would distract her, give her something to focus on other than him. Extracting butter, ham and a hunk of cheese, she plonked them on the table, then pulled off the lid of the bread crock and roughly hacked two slices to make the sandwich he'd demanded. Deliberately blank-faced, she handed it to him on a plate. He took it with an abstracted thank-you, and nodded at the colander full of strawberries that was on the draining board.

'Any chance of dessert?' he enquired.

Wordlessly, she scooped some into a bowl.

'Share them with me,' he invited. 'And let's eat outside. I'll take out one of these kitchen chairs for you.'

He hefted one up effortlessly and headed out for the garden, leaving a tight-lipped Sophie to follow him with the bowl of strawberries. She didn't want to share dessert with him. She didn't want to share anything with him—least of all her company. She wanted him to go. To stop disturbing her.

To leave her alone.

For ever.

Again.

She felt the knife slide into her side, a physical pain. Losing Nikos had been an agony.

He was never yours in the first place! Never! You were a fool—a selfish, stupid little fool! Weaving your infantile fantasies! Dreaming your puerile, egoistical happy ending to what was never real!

Angrily, she marched out into the garden, as if she could leave behind her tormenting thoughts. But the object of her torment was sitting himself down at the little table she had lugged out onto the tiny patio, getting stuck into the doorstep sandwich with every appearance of relish. The hot sun beat down, and he had taken off his jacket, hitching it around the back of the chair. Worse, he had dragged his tie loose and undone the top button of his shirt, loosening his cuffs and rolling back his sleeves, exposing his strong, lean forearms.

She felt her stomach hollow.

Oh, God, he looked so good! The whiteness of his shirt against the Mediterranean dusk of his skin tone. She wanted to gaze and gaze and gaze.

The way she had the first time she had ever set eyes on him. *Every* time she had ever set eyes on him.

What is it about him—what is that draws me to him?

Her thoughts were anguished, self-hating, and impossible to endure.

He glanced up at her. 'Come and sit down,' he said.

Her legs as weak as a kitten's, she sat, plonking down heavily on the chair. Her mind was in turmoil, her thoughts hopeless, jumbled, and as impossible to decipher as her maelstrom of emotions. She watched helplessly as he made short work of the sandwich. At least he wasn't looking back at her—that would have been unendurable. Instead he was looking around him at the little walled garden, his eyes taking in the difference between the pristine, dug-through areas she had been tackling and the untouched overgrown ones. Where she'd last been working was a pile of weeds, fast wilting in the afternoon sun beside her abandoned gardening tools.

Nikos frowned. 'You didn't have to do any of this,' he said abruptly.

What on earth had she done it for? It just didn't square with anything he'd expected. He'd expected to find her sulking, outraged at being relegated to this mouldering, deserted house, bored out of her pampered skin, itching for the bright lights, wanting someone—anyone—to spend some money on her! Wanting the easy life she'd always had, always wanted to keep…

His eyes hardened unconsciously. But not at his expense, thank you! He'd seen to that four years ago—and he was seeing to it now, as well. He'd settle her debts, but he was damned if she was going to get a luxury holiday, as well!

Yet as he gazed about him, seeing the evidence of hard manual labour all around him, he started to feel his thoughts shifting. They shifted even further when she answered him.

'I told you. I enjoy it,' she said tightly. 'It's very peaceful.'

Nikos's gaze snapped back to her. She didn't look like someone at peace—tension was visible in the set of her shoulders, the straightness of her back. His eyes worked over her, oblivious for the moment of the stiffening in her pose under his scrutiny. He still couldn't get over how totally different she looked from when he had last set eyes on her.

His eyes rested on her. She looked a million times better like this! Straggling hair, smut of dirt on her cheek, shabby T-shirt— none of it could distract from what was keeping his eyes on her.

Her beauty. Her sheer, extraordinary, breathtaking beauty! Her bones, her eyes, her mouth—all were just so…so…

He stopped analysing and just gazed, feeling an emotion go through him that seemed to be scouring him out from the inside. Memory kept pouring down into his consciousness— so many memories! Each one a vivid, vibrant picture in his head—of Sophie, Sophie, Sophie… So young, so beautiful… so magical…

Oh, she was older now, but her beauty had ripened, filled out, and without that tawdry mask of make-up it was as if he was seeing her all over again for the first time.

Abruptly she snapped her head away, sheering her gaze from him, her complexion paling beneath the honeyed hue that the summer sun had tinted her exposed skin with. The movement severed the moment. With a mental wrench, Nikos pushed aside his empty plate and reached for one of the luscious ruby strawberries glistening in their bowl. The warm ripeness was lush on his tongue, and he focussed on savouring it—blocking out as best he could his urge to scrutinise Sophie again.

Leave her alone! There's no point at all in looking…she's not for you, ever again!

But his thoughts seemed to be ringing hollow in his brain. Oh, he knew the score, all right—how could he not? He'd ripped Sophie Granton from him four long years ago, and he had no intention—none whatsoever—of letting her take root again. None. The hell with what he'd felt when he'd seen her again! That disastrous, fatal flash of desire. That had to be killed again, stone dead.

Which was exactly why he'd come to see her. Not because he wanted to see her again—never that!—but simply to drive home to her that, pay her debts he might, but pamper her he would *never* do! She'd have to put up with being dumped here, with all the privations it entailed, however much she resented it!

Except that she didn't seem to be resenting it….

Seemed, indeed, to have made herself at home here—humble though it was, self-reliant though she had to be. Seemed, indeed, to have got stuck in, quite unnecessarily, to diligent peasant labour! And found it peaceful!

Nikos found his gaze going out again over the garden. But then it *was* peaceful….

Warm and sunny and somnolent, with bees buzzing and birds chirruping. Unconsciously he reached for another strawberry, savouring again its sweet ripeness. He felt his muscles relax, and out of nowhere a sense of well-being start to steal over him. He stretched his long legs out and crossed them at the ankle, hooking an arm around the back of the chair as he continued with the strawberries. Across the table he could see Sophie's fingers reach out tentatively, stiffly, and take a strawberry for herself.

'They're very good,' he remarked. 'Are they from that bed over there?' He nodded in the direction.

'Yes,' she answered. 'They're ripening every day now. I had to clear away the weeds first.'

'Well worth it,' responded Nikos. His eye was drawn as a bird darted down to the pile of weeds and hopped on to the bared earth, pecking suddenly.

'What's that?' he enquired lazily, indicating the bird with his hand.

'It's a robin. It's after the grubs and worms in the soil. It's been dropping in every day. It's probably got a nest somewhere.' She was trying to talk normally, but it was hard. Harder still to go on sitting here, tense and awkward, while just across from her Nikos was stretching out in all his masculine glory, making himself at home, replete and relaxed.

Why can't he just go away? Why can't he clear off and leave me alone?

But the anguished rhetoric sounded hollow. Her sense, her sanity, might want him to disappear, but there was a part of her—a weak, dangerous part of her—that only wanted to let her gaze rest on him again, now that he was no longer looking at her, and gaze and gaze and gaze…

Feast on him even as he was feasting on the strawberries she'd picked.

'Feeding her chicks?' mused Nikos.

'*His* chicks,' she corrected. 'That's the male.'

'How can you tell?' His enquiry was as lazily voiced as his pose was relaxed.

'His red breast. Very handsome. Pulls the females.' There was a tart note in her voice.

Nikos gave a low chuckle. His gaze flicked to hers.

Mistake.

Mistake, mistake, mistake.

Nikos smiling—laughing. How many times had she seen him smiling at her, laughing with her? Her breath caught.

Oh, God, don't let me remember—don't let me remember!

She stifled the memories, fought them back. Fought just as hard against the tug of unstoppable attraction that pulled like a rope, lassoing her. Four years had only made him even more devastating, more magnetically compelling!

'So what do the females look like?' His question pulled her round.

'Very dull. Brown. Boring. Plain.'

He cocked an eyebrow again. 'How curious that nature is so different from humans. With us, it is the female who lures with her beauty—the male is the dull one, the plain one.'

Her eyes went to him. *Not you! Never, never you!*

She shifted in her seat, taking yet another strawberry. Focussing on that, not on him.

'So, tell me, what do you think of the place?' His query came invitingly, at odds with his former riling provocation.

'What?' She looked across at him again.

He took another strawberry too. 'You've been here four days—what do you make of the place? I take it you've wandered around? Not just confined yourself to this small garden? So, what do you think? Who knows? Once I've restored it and it's a hotel you might stay here one day.'

He spoke lightly, nonchalantly. But even as he did so he could suddenly see in his mind's eye Sophie as a guest at the hotel. A thought stabbed at his mind—what if there were no blighted past between them? What if he were to meet her at the hotel in the future for the first time? Attraction, unfettered by poisonous memories, flared in him.

How can she be so beautiful, even making no effort, like now, so full of natural grace that I cannot take my eyes from her?

His eyes rested on her, and Sophie felt her emotions plunge wildly, her breath catch. *No, he mustn't have that effect on me any more—he mustn't!*

But then he was getting to his feet, polishing off the last strawberry as he did so. He held a hand out to her. 'Come and tell me what you like about the place and what you don't,' he said.

He was holding out a hand to her. Almost, *almost* she put hers into it, as if taking his hand were nothing at all. Once holding Nikos's hand had been bliss itself. Now it would be nothing less than torture.

She got haltingly to her feet. Nikos was gesturing towards the garden door that led through into the main grounds. Numbly, she let herself be ushered out. Self-consciousness burned through her. They gained the terrace reaching along the front façade, and her gait was still stiff and awkward, then rounded the corner to the carriage sweep that led up to the grand front entrance. Skewed across the weed-infested gravel was a sight that brought her to a sudden halt.

She recognised it instantly—it was the same high-powered, low-slung car that he had been driving the very first day she'd ever set eyes on him. The exact same—she knew, because she'd become so besotted with him she'd learned the make, model and number plate. Memory overwhelmed her—

the first time she'd seen him, driving along the street to her father's house. The first time she'd been in the car herself.

And the last.

The time when he'd been driving her home late that last night, when her heart had been pounding with what she had been intending to do, her hands clammy with nerves.

And the sound of its engine had been the last noise she'd heard as he'd roared off into the night, leaving her weeping, demented, destroyed—clinging to the wall after he'd peeled her from him like a dirty rag...

'You've got the same car.'

The words broke from her before she could stop them. Nikos twisted his head, pausing in his stride. She'd gone pale again, pale beneath the flush of the honey-tan that was already gilding her fair skin.

She'd been pale as milk when he'd first met her. Long hours indoors, in music studios, had made her as fair as porcelain. His hand on hers had been striking in its contrast, with its olive Mediterranean skin.

Not just his hand on her hand.

Her breasts as white as snow, her limbs like ivory, as she pressed against him, as he crushed her to him, all sense swept away from him, all sanity gone—only the heady paradise of the senses...

'It's become a collector's item. Why update it when I can only legally use a fraction of its horsepower anyway?' His voice broke cuttingly across his thoughts.

'You let it rip at that racetrack you took me to.' Again the words were out of her mouth even as the memory formed in her mind.

Herself standing at the trackside, heart in her mouth as she watched him roaring along the straight, then tightening into

*a curve so punishing she thought he must surely career onto
the grass. Her heart filled with an exhilaration she could not
contain, an exhilaration that had consumed her completely,
when he'd taken her with him on the next lap, her breath
punctuated by gasps of terror and excitement, all the time
glorying in his skill, his strength, in the way he seemed so effortlessly to control the power of the car. She had thrilled to
it all, thrilled to him...*

Nikos's eyes went to hers. For a second, a fraction of a second, they met and held. Then he pulled his gaze away.

'Let's take a look at the grounds first.'

He started off down a wide but overgrown pathway.
Hesitantly Sophie followed him. The broad lawns were
hayfields, stretching either side, and the once elegantly
planted herbaceous borders had almost disappeared into the
overgrowth.

But there was beauty here, all right.

'There's so much work to do!' Sophie found herself ex-
claiming.

Nikos glanced back. 'Too much for you, I think.' But it was
not an admonition—there was a wry smile on his mouth.

It tugged at Sophie, and she glanced away. *No—please, not
this. Not feeling his power again! Please no!*

'I think it would take half a dozen professional gardeners,'
she made herself respond. She kept her voice light. It seemed
the safest thing to do.

'More like a dozen,' replied Nikos dryly. He paused as the
pathway diverged. 'I take it you've explored already?' he
said. 'Any suggestions?'

'There's a lake of sorts to the left. There's not much water in
it, from what I could see. Irises and bulrushes have taken over.'

'Let's take a look,' said Nikos. He strode off.

Numbly, she followed him. In part of her mind she knew that it was bizarre in the extreme for her to be exploring these neglected gardens with Nikos Kazandros.

Unreal.

And yet the reality of it was vivid. Far, far too vivid—

'You were right—it's hardly a lake at all any more.' Nikos's voice penetrated her thoughts. 'This will call for dredging. All the same…' He paused, scanning around him. 'It will be spectacular one day.'

His gaze came round to Sophie again.

'Did I do well, buying this place?'

There was humour in his voice and warmth in his eyes. She felt the breath squeeze in her lungs.

For a moment she did not move—could not. Only let her gaze be held by him, only let herself be warmed by the warmth in his eyes.

Once he looked at me like that all the time….

An ache started in her. She pulled her gaze away.

'It's very beautiful,' she said. There was constraint in her voice now.

Did he feel the same? He must, for abruptly he turned away, checking out a stand of ash saplings that had invaded from the woods beyond the lake.

'Those will have to go,' he said. 'And we'll need more specimen trees planted.'

We…

The ache in her side intensified. There was no 'we'. There never could be—never again.

She blinked. Nikos turned back. His eyes flickered over her, but she kept her expression veiled.

'Time to see the house,' he announced. His tone was brisk, businesslike.

Dutifully, Sophie followed him back through the long grass, up to the crumbling terrace.

'This way,' he said, and walked up to the door, fishing the keys from his trouser pocket, walking more quickly than he needed to. Briskly, he opened the front door of the house. The lock was stiff, but the door opened smoothly enough, even though the movement brought a strand of a cobweb floating down. He stepped inside, nostrils wrinkling at the dusty smell, and gazed around him.

Yes, he was right to have bought this place. On the verge of ruin it might be, but it was a gem of a house! Neglect and deterioration could not disguise the elegance of its proportions, nor the beauty of its interior. The moulding around the ceiling edge, the sweeping rise of the staircase, the dusty chandeliers suspended from the high central rose all testified to that.

'So, what do you think?'

He half turned. Sophie was in the doorway, looking up and about her. She hadn't seen the hall from this perspective before, and it was stunning.

'It's wonderful,' she said. The words came out spontaneously as she craned her head, gazing upwards.

Nikos stopped looking at the beautiful proportions of the hall—another set of beautiful proportions were riveting his gaze. Sophie's slender body was outlined in the sunlight filtering down through the high-set windows above the front door, making a halo around her hair. The exquisite line of her profile, the bow of her slightly parted mouth, the arched line of her throat, the gentle swell of her breasts all made his breath catch. He could not look away. Could not.

How does she do it? How?

Warning bells sounded inside his head, but he ignored

them. Ignored, too, the warning words sounding there—*be careful, be careful...*

Instead he went on gazing, feeling emotion uncoil inside him as if from a long, long sleep of many years.

Then her gaze swept round and down, and back to him—and pulled away, breaking the moment.

'Can you see this place as a hotel?' he asked.

Her expression flickered a moment under the impact of his regard, then steadied, darting about a moment to take in the space around her.

'Not really,' she said slowly. 'It's just a beautiful grand house.' Her brow furrowed slightly. 'Who lived here?' She'd wondered that on her earlier explorations, finding it sad that it was so clearly no longer inhabited.

'A very elderly widow who'd married the owner and lived here for fifty years with him before he died. Her nephew inherited and wanted to sell.'

'Fifty years?' Sophie echoed. So many years of marriage! She felt her heart contract. So beautiful a house to live in, for so long! In her head burned, betrayingly, the thought that had pierced her the day she'd wandered around on her own. *We could have lived here, Nikos and me...our own private paradise...*

But paradise had not been waiting for her. Neither with Nikos nor without. To purge the traitorous thought, she made herself go on. 'I'm sure it could be done up to make it work as a hotel,' she said.

'It has to be restored very carefully, with scrupulous period detail,' Nikos replied, his gaze working methodically, assessing all that needed doing. 'The historical architect who is to be in charge was to have met me here this afternoon. He's been delayed until tomorrow. I'm staying overnight at a local inn. You're in the only habitable part of the house.'

Sophie could only stare. 'Oh,' was all she could say. Dismay filled her, and more complex emotions too. Disturbing emotions.

He was opening doors now, looking inside the rooms opening off the hallway, pausing as if to make mental notes, but Sophie did not follow him. Only when he headed further into the interior of the hallway, beyond the staircase, did she follow him. A moment later she wished she had stayed where she was. Nikos had opened the double doorway to the music room. The covered bulk of the grand piano was instantly visible. He turned to look back at her.

'Something of a find for you—though, I take it it's out of tune?' There was a timbre to his voice she didn't want there. He was acknowledging a past where once the presence of such an instrument would have had her trying it out instantly. But no longer.

She spoke tightly. 'I've no idea.'

He raised an eyebrow. 'Surely you couldn't resist playing it?'

'I don't play any more.' Her voice was terse. Her mouth tight-lipped.

A frown creased between his eyes. 'So much for the dedicated music student,' he remarked caustically.

Of its own volition Sophie's throat constricted. Parting with her piano had caused almost more anguish than having to sell the house. But her baby grand had been worth money, and money was all that she had allowed herself to focus on.

Nikos was looking at her, she realised. Frowningly.

'I thought your music meant everything to you. What made you give it up?'

She could not answer him. Turning away, she stumbled blindly towards the baize door that led to the servants' quarters. He strode after her, catching her arm to stay her. It burned like a brand and she pulled free. He caught at her again, catching her hand. Then abruptly he frowned, lifting her hand into the light and turning it over, seizing her other hand at the same time before she could stop him.

He was staring down at them, his frown deepening, while she tried desperately not to feel the touch of his cool fingers on her or feel the closeness of his body to hers.

'They're scratched to pieces!' he exclaimed.

'It's just from gardening,' she answered faintly. Again she tried to pull them away from him, but it did not make him let them go. Instead he smoothed his thumbs over her palms.

'You should look after them more.' His voice had softened, like his touch. Sophie's stomach hollowed. The tone of his voice and the slow smoothing of his thumbs sent a thousand nerve endings sussurating.

He was speaking again, with the same timbre in his tone. 'You always had such beautiful hands. You kept them as soft as silk. Your touch was like velvet…'

There was a husk in his voice. He was too close—way, way too close to her. Her hands were like imprisoned birds in his—birds that he was soothing, captivating. Her heart was thudding, slow and heavy, her breaths were shallow and uneven. Dear God, she couldn't be here—she couldn't! Couldn't let him caress her palms like that—couldn't let herself respond. Couldn't. Mustn't.

Somehow she had to break free, stop him…stop herself…

'Nikos,' she breathed. Her eyes fluttered to his. 'Let me go…'

The tall bulk of his body was too close to hers, the spiced, heady scent of his skin too overpowering. She could see everything about him—everything. The darkening line of his jaw, the sculpted shape of his mouth, the blade of his nose and the dark, drowning eyes.

'Let me go…'

It was a whisper. A plea.

Something moved in his eyes. They were alone in the house, alone in the world. And far, far too close—

'I can't,' he said, his eyes pouring into hers.

As he spoke the words he knew them for the truth. The hopeless, stark truth. Slowly, infinitely slowly, his grip on her hands tightened, drawing her closer towards him, closer still. His mouth started to lower to hers…

'I can't resist you.' His voice was nothing but a husk. 'Sophie…'

There was longing in his voice, a caress.

Panic beat up in her—panic and more—much, much more! For a moment she was poised between the two, almost yielding to his voice, his touch, to his mouth so close to hers…

With despairing sanity, she freed herself. She stared blindly, her face aghast at what had so very nearly happened. Then, as if impelled by a reflex so urgent it possessed her totally, she pushed roughly past, tugging at the baize door and then hurtling down the stone-flagged corridor beyond, her footsteps echoing in the empty house.

Behind her, Nikos stood stock still.

What had he nearly done?

For a moment he, too, was poised in the balance, between what had so nearly happened and the hollowing realisation flooding through him now.

I nearly kissed her—

How had he let himself get so close to such a thing?

But he knew how—knew utterly. He'd wanted to kiss her. Feel for one long, blissful moment her soft lips beneath his…

Shudderingly, he pulled his mind away, banned it from the path it sought to follow. No! No, he must not allow this! Sophie was the past—the poisoned, tormented past. She was not the present—she must not be! Yet he had come *that* close to kissing her! That close to taking her slender, pliant body in his willing arms and kissing her…

With stringent effort, he sheered his thoughts away again. This had to stop! Now—right now! He should leave—right away—and never, *never* come near her again!

But would that stop him thinking about her? At his sides, his hands balled into fists. Four years ago, it had cost him more than he could bear to stop himself thinking about Sophie, by day and by night. And now—now that he stood so close to the edge of the cliff he had hauled himself up, hand over hand, so arduously four years ago—would he not be back exactly where he had once been?

I have to make myself immune to her! I have to see her as simply an ordinary woman, no one special. Beautiful, yes, but nothing more than that!

But how to make himself immune? As he stood, with the silent, deserted house all around him, it came to him. The logic clear and simple. Obvious. Slowly he felt his hands unfist. Of course! *That* was what he must do! *That* was his way out of this impossible impasse! He wanted immunity to her—well, the way to achieve it was staring him in the face! Immunity was achieved by exposure—that was how it worked. You exposed yourself to the infection and you gained immunity to it. If it worked with disease, it would work with the lethal vulnerability to Sophie Grafton that he was infected with!

As his hands unfisted he felt the tension drain out of him. Of *course* that was what he must do. Desensitise himself to her by treating her as if she were anyone—someone quite ordinary. Someone who had never had the disastrous impact on him that she had once had. Someone he could spend time with as easily, as uncomplicatedly, as any other person.

Over dinner, for example.

Yes, that was what he would do—he would take her to dinner tonight. A few hours in her company, in a public place, and he would soon be desensitised to her. See her not as a ghost from his past but as just a dinner companion, one of so many in his life. He would take from her the power to haunt him.

Resolution filled him. He glanced at his watch. By the end of the evening his purpose would have been achieved. Immunity from a woman he must never, never allow himself to desire again.

CHAPTER SEVEN

SOPHIE was tearing up weeds. Ruthlessly, urgently. As if pulling weeds out of her own heart. Weeds that had the face of Nikos Kazandros! Emotion scythed through her. Dear God, how close, how perilously, disastrously close she had come to letting him kiss her—

Kiss her! Just like that—there and then!

She had so nearly let it happen! Nearly let herself yield to him! The strength it had taken to pull away, back to safety, to sanity, had been almost beyond her! But she'd done it, and thank God for it!

Gradually, as she worked, her heart-rate slowed and she started to calm, to regain some shred of composure. It was all right. She was safe. He hadn't come after her. He was leaving her alone. And when she heard, a short time later, the throaty roar of Nikos's car, she felt safer yet. Safer still if she didn't let herself dwell on what had nearly happened. Safer if she kept herself doggedly working, until the shadows lengthened across the whole garden, and her back was aching, and she knew she needed to stop.

Stiffly, she got to her feet. There was sun now only in the treetops, high above. The walled garden itself was completely in the shade. She gave a little shiver. It was cool to the point of chill. And as she looked around the shadows seemed to bring a pall of melancholy sifting over her—a sense of slow, abandoned desolation.

She was alone. Completely alone. Nikos was long gone. And, for a reason she did not want to think about, she felt suddenly bereft.

For a moment she just stood there, staring bleakly. Then, as she knew she must—for what else could she do?—she squared her shoulders and went indoors.

She would fill the evening ahead as she had filled all those up till now. She would wash, make herself some supper, and watch something on TV—whatever was on, she didn't care much—then go to bed. And she would *not* think herself lonely, the evening ahead empty...

No—she must not allow herself to feel like this! She'd been content enough alone here up till now! Relishing the peace, the silence, the beauty of nature all around. So why, now, should she think she felt alone...restless?

So empty.

So desolate.

She felt tears prick behind her eyelids, but she blinked them away. She would not cry, *must* not cry, for something that was was impossible. It had been impossible four years ago and it still was—always would be. There was nothing in her life now but the endless grind of doing what she had to do, whatever it took.

With an indrawn breath she would not admit was heavy, she got on with washing the dirt off her hands, wincing slightly at the scratches.

He held my hands, soothed them with his—

No—the shutter sliced down again. Roughly, she dried

her hands, flexing her shoulders to loosen them up. But just as she was replacing the hand towel she stilled, every nerve suddenly alert.

It was a car, coming along the drive. And the low, throaty note was all too familiar. Her thoughts churned wildly, but before she could even think coherently the car had drawn to a loud halt by the back door. She heard the engine cut, a door slam. Then Nikos was at the kitchen door, walking right in.

Sophie froze, silenced completely. Inside, she felt her pulse kick into hectic life.

'I've come to take you out to dinner,' Nikos announced.

For a timeless moment Sophie could only stare up at him. *'Dinner?'*

'Yes. I've made a reservation at the inn I'm staying at. It's a few miles off, but not too far.' He spoke as if taking her to dinner were the most natural thing in the world.

She couldn't speak. Could only stare and swallow help-lessly. Then she found words.

'I can't go to dinner with you.' It was baldly said, but inside her head her mind was flailing helplessly, incapable of thought, of rational comprehension. Overwhelming her was emotion.

It was Nikos! Nikos back again—standing right here, right in front of her. Telling her he was taking her to dinner.

A dark eyebrow tilted upwards at her words. 'You have another engagement?' he posed.

She felt herself flush. 'Of course not. But that doesn't mean I can just—'

'Why not?' he interrupted. 'After all, you've been living on short rations for a few days—you must be keen for some more sophisticated fare by now!'

'I'm perfectly OK here,' she riposted.

'Well, now you can have a decent dinner anyway, can't you?' He glanced at her attire. 'You'll need to change, though.'

'I haven't anything suitable for going out,' she answered. In her mind, painfully, sprang the memory of the extensive wardrobe she had once enjoyed. Every item had long gone.

'It doesn't matter,' he said. 'There's no dress code at the restaurant.'

It wasn't the answer she wanted. 'Nikos, this is…' she began. *Mad*, she wanted to say. *Insane. Pointless.* But the words didn't come. Helplessly, she fell silent.

'Go and change,' he prompted. 'Don't be too long—I only had a sandwich for lunch, remember!'

There was light humour in his voice, and she wondered at it. She was still trying to make sense of what was happening. Why on earth was he here to take her to dinner? It was incomprehensible.

It was unbearable.

Her mouth twisted briefly. But then the last four years had taught her that the unbearable still had to be borne…

This was just one more thing that she had to endure. And that was what she would have to do this evening. Get through it. Endure it. Endure the torment of having dinner with Nikos…

Numbly, she found herself turning round and heading upstairs to the little bedroom over the sitting room.

Below, Nikos felt his breath draw in.

Was he really doing the right thing? He silenced his doubts. He'd been through them all since driving away earlier. This *was* the right thing to do. Somehow he had to make himself immune to Sophie, so that she was no longer haunting him from the past. So that he could see her again and feel nothing about her. Nothing at all.

He could hear her upstairs, the creaking floorboards revealing her activity. She didn't keep him long, and he could hear the tread of her footsteps coming downstairs as he was locking the garden door. She hadn't been exaggerating when she had said she had nothing suitable with her—the blouse and skirt she had changed into, though neat and clean, were clearly daywear. Her hair had been simply clipped back into a low ponytail, and she had not bothered with make-up. Well, he told himself bluntly, it was all to the good if she weren't dressed up. The last thing he wanted was her exacerbating her natural beauty in any way whatsoever.

The gypsy skirt she was wearing the first time I set eyes on her, swirling around her long, long legs… The peach dress she wore to dinner that evening, accentuating every pliant line of her body… The ivory evening gown she wore to that gala, the first night I took her out…

Through his head she walked like a procession, each vision a wound. Roughly, he banished them. They were the past, and the past was over. Now, only the immunisation programme was ahead of him. Nothing else.

He led the way out to the car, and opened the passenger seat. For a moment she seemed to balk, then climbed in, settling the seat belt across her, her face inexpressive.

But behind the blank expression she was fighting down emotion. Crushing down the memories that tried to come crowding into her head. *Don't think…don't remember.* It was all she could do, all she could tell herself. *And don't, above all, look at the man sitting beside you, his powerful frame so close you could almost brush your sleeve against his.*

As Nikos gunned the engine she felt the G-force thrust her back in her seat. He drove as he had always driven, with ultra-masculine assurance, and the powerful car creamed down the driveway and out on to the public highway, revving strongly as he roared through the quiet countryside. To distract her flailing emotions she looked about her, at rolling fields and woodland, anywhere but at the man driving her. Where they were she still had no idea, and didn't care anyway.

After about ten minutes he pulled off the main road and drew up in front of a prosperous-looking inn, with mullioned windows, overhanging eaves, and flower boxes along the sills. It looked pretty and old and immaculately kept. Judging by the kind of up-market cars parked, it was clearly the kind of place that attracted a well-heeled clientele.

They went inside, Nikos ducking his head as they stepped into the old-world interior. As always, as Sophie remembered, he received instant attention, and within a few minutes they were installed at a spacious table set inside a glassed-in extension to the rear of the building, overlooking a close-mown lawn that stretched down to a little river. Cool air wafted in from wide-open French windows.

Sophie sat, feeling mixed emotions trying to jostle their way past the glaze she had forcibly imposed on herself since the moment she had climbed into Nikos's car. Why Nikos was doing this she had no idea. Her only priority was to get through this ordeal intact.

But it was going to be torture to endure his company, to have to go through the hideous mockery of dining with him as if they were actually a couple….

As once they had been….

No—stop that! Stop it now—right now. She said the words to herself fiercely, inside her head.

Just shake the napkin on to your lap, smile at the waiter, look through the menu, make a choice—any choice; it doesn't matter—then put the menu aside, pick up your glass of water, look out of the window, look at the river, the lawn, the flowers, the countryside. Look at anything, anything at all, but don't look at Nikos…don't look at Nikos—

Her eyes went to him. Hopelessly, helplessly. How could she do anything else except look at him? Look at the perfect sculpture of his face; its every contour known to her, every glance, every expression, an image on her very heart—once, so long, long ago.

But no longer. And never again. That was what she had to remember. All she could permit herself to think.

With a silent intake of breath she shifted her eyes away as he studied the menu, reached instead, idly, for the little card that sat within the centrepiece of the table, flanked by pepper and salt and a tastefully arranged spray of flowers. She glanced at the card, with its printed sketch of the front of the inn and the address. They were somewhere in Hampshire, so it seemed, close to a village Sophie had never heard of. It didn't seem particularly important to her where she was, so she replaced the card. Then, resolutely, she turned her head to look out over the view again.

'Sophie?'

Her head snapped round. Nikos was looking at her, one eyebrow quirked questioningly. A waiter had materialised beside the table and was clearly ready to take their order. She swallowed, and murmured her requests, then Nikos gave his.

He was choosing lamb for his entrée, and memory stabbed at her. It had always been his favourite, and she could vividly remember him telling her about all the traditional Greek methods of cooking lamb, baking it so slowly that the meat fell from the bones because it was so tender.

'You must come to Greece—then you will see,' he had said. And she had felt her heart give a little lift, as though it were already on its way to heaven. Why would he take her to

Greece except to meet his parents, introduce her as the girl he loved, wanted to marry? Oh, please, *please* let it be so! She had loved him so much, so much—

Her mind sheered away. She had never gone to Greece with him.

And she no longer loved him.

He had killed her love for him—stabbed her to the heart. And she had handed him the dagger with which to do it. And her life had shattered to pieces.

A heaviness crushed down on her. An old, familiar bitterness.

He was handing back the leather-bound menus, turning his attention to the wine list, relaying his decision to the hovering *maître d'*. Then his attention turned to Sophie. She lifted her chin. She would not look away. She would bear this and stick it out. Why he was going through this farce she could not begin to guess, but she would not crumble. His expression seemed veiled, as though he were hiding some emotion behind the dark surface of his eyes. Despite her intention to stay unperturbed, she found herself reaching jerkily for her water glass.

'Sophie—'

She stayed her hand. Swallowed. 'Yes?'

He seemed uncertain for a moment, then he spoke. 'Sophie, the reason I'm having dinner with you is this. I want to draw a line under the past. I don't want it intruding again. You clearly don't, either. So I want to have an evening with you that proves to us both that, in the unlikely event of our paths ever crossing again, they can do so without the drama that has happened this time.'

He took a breath, then went on, his voice crisp and decisive. 'I trust, with your debt settled, your financial problems are now averted. You got yourself into a dangerous mess, but you're out of it now, and I'm sure you'll have the good sense not to consider that dire option a sensible course ever to consider again. Now, I've lectured you quite enough—' he permitted himself a lightening of his brisk tone '—so let us change the subject and not refer to it again.'

She was looking at him strangely as he spoke, a closed look on her face. He wondered at it fleetingly, and then the wine waiter was there, proffering the bottle he'd selected. Once the tasting and the pouring were complete, he lifted his filled glass and took a contemplative mouthful. Replacing the glass, he remarked, his tone conversational, 'So, you decided music wasn't for you after all?'

'No.' There was no emotion in her voice and she did not elaborate.

She wasn't going to be forthcoming, clearly, and Nikos let it be. Her defection from a subject she had once been devoted to surprised him, but perhaps her vaunted devotion to her music had been as shallow as other aspects of her character.

He pulled his thoughts away from that dark path. He was not going there. Tonight was about the future, not the past. And the future was about making Sophie Granton nothing more than a passing acquaintance to whom he had total immunity.

He started again, making his tone conversational once more. 'What did you take up instead to occupy you?'

Carefully, Sophie picked up her wineglass. The tips of her fingers were white.

'Nothing much,' she said.

It was like getting blood out of a stone, thought Nikos.

Once they had talked with eager fluency, never at a loss, talking of anything and everything.

The first course was served, and Nikos was glad, but as they started to eat, he resumed his attempts.

'What sort of "nothing much"?' He smiled.

Sophie forked up a morsel of her seafood concoction, savouring its delicate flavour. It took her mind off Nikos's relentless probing.

'I work,' she answered.

His eyebrows rose. If she were in paid employment she had clearly failed to live within her salary, running up debts that she'd resorted to trying to pay with that vile escort work.

'What sort of work?' He kept his voice pleasantly enquiring.

'In a shoe shop.' It was the truth—or had been until she'd not turned up the day she'd been driven here. She doubted the shop would take her back, and that would mean another dispiriting trip to the unemployment office, trying to find something, anything, that kept money coming in, however low paid. Nikos's five thousand pound loan had only bought her a limited amount of time. Nothing more than that.

For a moment she felt fear, so familiar, so terrifying, bite in her throat. Dear God, how could she keep going? Doing what she had to do—had no choice but do?

Surviving—I'm surviving. Day after day. Week after week. It's all I can do and I have to go on doing it. Scraping together the money that I need. That I go on needing. And there's nothing I can do except to go on doing what I'm doing.

'Ah…' Nikos understood now. It was a popular option, working in a fashionable boutique, especially when the shop was owned by a friend and run as a little hobby—something to occupy women like her, to while away the time. 'That must be useful if you want to snap up the latest designs first,' he remarked lightly.

He named a couple of top shoe designers, the likes of which had never been seen in the downmarket, off-the-rack shoe shop Sophie had worked at every day of the week, morning through late opening. Except for the two precious afternoons a week she'd insisted on taking off, that made her whole bleak existence, her endless, punishing struggle for survival, worthwhile.

Nikos saw her face shutter again. Did she just not want to talk about herself to him at any level? Even the mundanely conversational? Well, OK then, he would back off even from that. He could understand if she were touchy about anything personal.

Determinedly, he tried another gambit.

'It was good of you to tackle the walled garden as you did. The gardens, I think, are going to be as great a challenge as the house to restore! Fortunately I understand that the original landscape designs drawn up for Belledon in the eighteenth century are still existing, so they will guide the work.'

Sophie reached for her wine. She felt the alcohol slide into her system and was grateful.

'Belledon?'

'Your accommodation,' he clarified. 'Although you may not see it as a hotel, it is highly suitable, all the same, for such use. It's within five miles of the motorway from Heathrow and, fully restored, will be a showpiece for the area. I envisage it will be one of the leading country house hotels in the UK, despite the cost of its restoration.'

He warmed to his theme, and Sophie was glad of it— grateful he had abandoned his unbearable inquisition of her. She let him talk, busying herself eating the delicious food. It would be foolish and wasteful not to make the most of it. The first course had been removed, and a succulent fillet of lamb placed in front of each of them.

'This is good,' approved Nikos. 'Locally sourced, so the menu says. The Belledon chef will have to be on his mettle, I can see! Fortunately the home farm is part of the estate, and it will supply the bulk of the food for the hotel. The kitchen garden you have been so energetically restoring will also contribute significantly. Ideally, I would like all the food to be organic, although it will take time to achieve certification. But it is something to work towards.'

Again, he went on talking as they ate, and without realising it Sophie found herself being drawn into the conversation. The level of wine in her glass seemed constant, though she was not aware of it being refilled. But she could feel the alcohol entering her bloodstream, warming it. Dissolving, slowly but steadily, thread by thread, the net of tension webbing her at being here with Nikos. But so, too, was the conversation, she realised. As Nikos talked on about the intricacies and challenges of restoring an historic country house, ranging from one aspect to another, she found herself taking a real interest in the undertaking. Unconsciously she started to ask questions, make observations, volunteer opinions.

With part of her mind she wondered at it. Wondered at herself being here, like this, with Nikos, listening to him, talking to him, sharing a meal with him. As if, she realised, with a mix of emotions piercing her, there were no tormented history between them. As if, impossible though it must surely be, she were simply being wined and dined by him. As if there was nothing dark nor desperate poisoning the air. As if—and this surely must be an illusion—could only be an illusion— as if the heavy, crushing pall of the past that had weighed down on her was lifting away….

It was not real. She knew that. Knew it was only an illusion—an illusion brought on by the sense of unreality enmeshing her at being here, having dinner with Nikos, having him sitting opposite her, so close she could have reached out to him, touched his hand, his face. So close she could see the indentation around his mouth when he gave his quick smile, the gold flecks in his eyes as his expression became animated at the subject he was talking about, the silky sable fall of his hair across his well-shaped forehead. Yet, illusion though it was, illusion though it must be, she knew she could not deny what it offered her.

A respite—however brief, however illusory—from the endless torment in her head that Nikos evoked.

He'd said he wanted to draw a line under the past. It had seemed, when he'd uttered it, an impossible thing to do! And yet now, as the meal progressed and the conversation flowed so effortlessly, across subjects that were blessedly free of anything sensitive, anything personal, she was finding herself wondering whether it could be done. She felt the landscape of her emotions shift again, altering everything subtly, silently. It was not that the past had disappeared, but it was a different part of the past that was in her mental vision now, it seemed. Not the bitter, tormented past that had scarred and scoured her, but the past that this evening now recalled and echoed.

Familiarity rushed through her. How many times had she and he sat together, talking about everything, anything, the flow of conversation easy, stimulating, engaging, enthralling? This was Nikos as she remembered him in those golden days she had spent with him, with time flashing by, his keen mind a foil to hers, his ready laugh, his easy smile—

Because it had never, never just been his incredible looks that had captivated her—it had been so much more. The sheer pleasure of his company, the ease, the companionship…

Emotion tugged at her—a poignancy she could not avert. She felt it running through her veins like a darting arrow. How much she had lost in losing him! How *much!*

Yet counterpointed to the sense of loss was for now, for this fleeting, brief time, a sense of something so precious that she felt it was like a jewel nestled in her palm. However fleeting this evening was, however illusory, that sense of bitterness was washed away, and the time now was real. However fleeting, she would be grateful for it, glad for it—drinking the sweet, heady wine that it offered her to the very last.

Outside, the evening had darkened into night, and the candle on the table threw its light on to the glass of the conservatory window, creating, as it did, a flickering parallel world. Sophie's eyes drifted towards it, and she felt her emotions quicken again—they were there, she and Nikos, in that parallel world of light and shadow, illuminated together.

Together…

The word pierced in her heart and she felt its power. There in that shadow world there had been no separation. In that shadow world there was no bitter past. There, in the illusory reality of the candle-light, it was as if they had always been like this—as if the years of parting had never been. She felt her mind run on, seizing a present that could never be out of a past that never was.

If we had never parted that could be us, there, in that other existence! That could be the reality, and these four long bitter years could have been the sweetest of all!

For precious moments she let herself revel in the sweetness of the thought, the beguiling, wondrous fantasy that she and Nikos were simply here together, man and wife, come down to visit his beautiful abandoned house, to plan its restoration, to fill it once more with life and love, envisage it as a place for them to live in. She and him…a family…a happiness to last a lifetime….

She knew it was not real, *could* not be real, and yet in her mind it was. In her mind as she sat there, sipping at her wine, eating the delicious morsels of food, and gazing, oh, just gazing—and gazing and gazing—at the man so close to her, it was all the reality she craved. All the reality she yearned for. The other reality, the one she had been condemned to, which weighed and crushed and pulled her down, had slipped away. Now there was only this sweet, wondrous reality. And it was enough…

Waiters came to clear the table, presenting her with a dessert menu. She chose randomly, and something duly appeared, together with a glass of sweet, delicate Beaune de Venise, which she sipped as she spooned up the delicious concoction before her. Her mind was getting hazy, but she didn't care. The outer world, her consciousness of it, seemed to be receding. A strange sense of dissociation drifted down on her. She found she could sit, sipping her sweet wine, and let Nikos's voice wind about her as her eyes rested on him. It was strange, so strange, she found herself thinking bemusedly. How she could just sit here…gazing at him. Taking him in…all his male perfection…her eyes drifting over him…

Nikos—only Nikos…only ever Nikos in all the world for me…

Her heart was full with emotion, the jewel in her palm rich and rare and so, so precious…

'Sophie?'

Her name sounded in the air, sibilant and questioning. Nikos was looking at her enquiringly, his chair half pushed back. The dining room was almost deserted, the candle burnt low. The couple in the glass had vanished.

Or had they?

She got to her feet, as Nikos did the same, and then he was there, ushering her out as they were bowed away by the waiter—the last diners to leave, she saw. And Nikos was at her side, falling in beside her, as they stepped through the open French windows into the garden beyond the conservatory restaurant. She felt his presence, his closeness. Felt the rightness of his place at her side.

This is where he should be—where I should be…

Like the couple in the glass. Together.

'Are you cold?' Nikos's enquiry was solicitous as he walked beside her on the dimly lit path.

Sophie shook her head. She wasn't cold. The wine in her veins and the soft summer night warmed her. So did the heat in her blood. Was her pulse heavier than it normally was? Or was she just more conscious of the beating of her heart?

More conscious of the tall figure at her side?

What am I doing here? she thought. Surely she could not be here, with Nikos, having dined with him, talked to him, listened to him. Reality was prickling at her mind, penetrating the hazy miasma that had been cocooning her. Yet its entrance was unsure, uncertain.

She glanced about her. What was real? The night air? The scent of honeysuckle teasing her senses? The fall of their footsteps on the path? The massed dimness at the edge of the garden?

Nikos at her side?

Could *he* be real?

Oh, yes—oh, yes… He was real!

Nikos—Nikos, Nikos…

She tried to silence the voice in her head, for it had no right to cry out like that—nor reason, either. But reasons seemed a thousand miles away, and all that was left was a burning consciousness of his presence—a consciousness that became even more vivid as he paused at the top of a short flight of steps, looking upwards into the sky.

'Look at the stars,' he said.

She followed his uplifted gaze. Overhead the heavens

shone, pricked with gold, the faintest wisps of cloud scudding over them.

'There's Jupiter,' he said.

She gazed blindly. He raised his hand, to point, and as he did so his other hand closed on her shoulder, to alter her position slightly. Suddenly his breath was warm on her neck, and the stars blurred in her eyes. The warmth of his palm on her shoulder seemed like a brand. Imprinting her with his presence.

For a moment, timeless and motionless, she stilled completely, every cell in her body piercingly aware of Nikos's closeness, his touch, his breath, his scent, his very being. Emotion lifted her.

Then, abruptly, the hand at her shoulder fell away.

'The car park is just through here,' he said. His voice was terse suddenly, and his pace as they walked towards the gate that led from the garden quickened. She felt the emotion that had lifted her hang, quiveringly, inside her.

As he gained the car, opening the passenger door for her, Nikos set his jaw tensely. What was happening to him?

What had been happening all evening?

As he gunned the engine and manoeuvred the car out of the car park, he tried to get his head around it. The evening had had a clear, unambiguous purpose: to put the past behind him. To make him see, finally, that the past was over and done with. That Sophie had no power to arouse emotions in him. That he could gain immunity from her, from what she could do to him…

Liar…

The word shaped itself in his head and he brushed it aside, but it reformed again. From the corner of his eye he could see her sitting there beside him, feel her presence, her reality.

Sophie…

Everything about her seemed so vivid, so vital! Everything about her was imprinted on him. In every cell of his body. Emotion washed through him. Emotion that *she* aroused! Only *she* aroused. Only Sophie…

Only Sophie….

The car ate up the few miles as he closed the distance to Belledon. They did not talk—yet the silence spoke. His head was full—but not with words, not with thoughts.

As he wound down the long drive to the house, took the curve around to the back and drew up outside the entrance to her quarters, he could feel the emotion in him strengthening. What it was he did not know, could not name. Knew only that it was strong and growing stronger. More imperative. More powerful.

I should leave. Leave her and go. Get back to the inn and then, first thing, head back to London. The architect can wait. He's not important. All that is important is for me to get back to London. Away.

Away from Sophie…

But even as the thought forced its way into his head he knew it for the lie it was.

He cut the engine and the silence pooled. With a jerky movement Nikos opened his door, strode out around the car to open the passenger seat door. She got out quickly, shutting the door herself. Nikos walked up to the back door, unlocking it with his own set of keys for the property. It took a moment to find the right key, but then it yielded, and he pushed the door back, holding it open for her.

He did not speak.

Dared not speak.

Dared not look at her.

She approached slowly. There was a sudden wariness in

her step. A sudden slow thump of her heart. All around was nothing but silence. Then the mournful cry of an owl pierced it momentarily.

'Sophie—'

The sound of his voice penetrated. Her eyes went to him as he stood in the dimness by the open door, waiting for her to go inside. Waiting to leave. To drive away. She paused. The air was chill now, after the warmth of the car, but it was not the night that chilled her.

Knowledge came to her.

I will never see Nikos again now.

He would drive away and she would never see him again.

She knew it with an absolute certainty. There would be no more accidental encounters, no more crossing of paths. No more.

A terrible yearning swept through her. A yearning for what had never been, for what never would be. What never could be.

With aching pain, she moved past him.

'Sophie—'

She paused minutely. She could not say goodnight, could not speak anodyne words. It was all beyond her.

'Sophie, I—'

She tilted her head—the barest acknowledgement. 'Goodbye, Nikos.'

Her voice was low, faint. She had meant to say goodnight, but a truer word had come. She started forwards again, into the interior.

'Sophie—'

Her name came from him again, but it was different now, and his hand was on her shoulder. Halting her. She turned.

He was so close to her. Standing there in the doorway, his hand on her shoulder, pressing through the material of her blouse. He said something in Greek. She did not know what. Knew only that in the darkness of the night his face was stark.

His eyes were burning suddenly, with a fire that came from deep within.

Weakness went through her, making her breath catch, her heart seize. The warmth of his hand on her shoulder made her weaker yet. Her eyes clung to his. Clung in desperation, beseeching. Yearning.

Oh, dear God—Nikos!

Emotion filled her that she should be so close to him, and then anguish that this was, could only be, her final moment with him. That nothing remained—only this final parting.

And then…

Slowly, infinitely slowly, as if a weight were dragging at him, his hands slid from her shoulders to fasten around her arms. She felt his muscles tense, felt him draw her towards him. Her heartbeat had slowed. Her breath stopped. Time stopped. The unbearable past that had taken him from her once, the unbearable future that would take him from her for ever, all vanished, and there was only this moment—now. This moment with him. The soft dark of the night, the dim points of the stars, the faint soughing of the wind in the distant trees, the haunting cry of the hunting owl—that was all there was.

And Nikos. So close to her. So close.

Holding her.

Words came from him again, in his own language, low and rasped. She did not understand. But she did not need words to know what was in his eyes, his face.

His lips.

In a slow, slow descent, his mouth covered hers.

Like silken velvet his mouth moved on hers, drawing from her a nectar sweeter than honey. The nectar he had tasted before, as sweet as this. The nectar that had been in her very first kiss—and in her last.

And now in this.

She opened to him. She could not do otherwise. Giving herself, all of herself, to this moment of bliss. Nikos kissing her. Nikos's mouth moving on hers softly, slowly.

As he had kissed her the very first time.

Past and present fused in her head, her heart. The past she had submerged beneath layer after layer of desperately imposed barriers was now as real and singing in her consciousness as the bliss of the present.

Holland Park, after the open-air opera, walking along, hand in hand, his fingers laced with hers. Nikos pausing in the shadowed pathway to turn her slowly towards him, to murmur her name, and then, as her eyes fluttered shut, to do what she had been longing, aching for him to do—kiss her...

It was as if that moment had come again—as if this was the first time all over again. As if her heart were singing, soaring as it had then, her body and soul filling with the sweetest bliss.

Then, in that distant, long-ago past, he had drawn back regretfully, reluctantly, and she had gone on standing there, dazed and dizzy with delight, gazing up at him, lips parted, her heart soaring heavenward on wings of wonder.

'*I must take you home,*' he'd murmured then, and had walked with her, slowly, his arm around her shoulders, their bodies touching. They had meandered homewards, slowly, back towards her father's house. His car had been parked there, and though she had invited him in for coffee—daringly, hopefully—he had ruefully shaken his head.

'*I can't,*' he'd said. '*Or I will want to stay...*'

All he'd done was tilt up her chin and drop the lightest,

slightest kiss upon her lips. Then he'd let her go and turned away, walked back to the car, pausing only to lift his hand in a final goodnight and call softly, 'Go in, Sophie.'

And she had, though it had been like tearing herself away, and when she had shut the front door she had leant back against it until she'd heard his car drive away, and then she had drifted upstairs, floating on air to her bedroom, aching with all her being for him.

As she ached now. Now that she was in his arms again— now that the bliss of his kiss was soaring in her veins—now that the low, hectic beat of her heart, the pulse of her blood, were binding her to him—now that the warm, sensuous pressure of his mouth was drowning her senses.

She gave herself to it absolutely, completely. Not even trying to fight, trying to resist. The past flowed into the present, becoming one.

He guided her to the staircase and up the narrow stairs, into the dim, encompassing darkness that awaited there. To take her into his arms again. The darkness enveloped them, but he did not need light to tell him what he knew—that her soft, slender body folded to his, that her tender, rounded breasts pressed against him, that her sweet, generous mouth was like honey beneath his. Nectar.

Did he speak? He did not know. Nor if he spoke Greek or English. Knew only that his hand had slipped around the nape of her neck, cradling her head to his as his other hand slid down the long wand-curve of her spine. He was kissing her still, deeper, and yet each kiss only engendered a greater hunger, a wilder desire for her. His fingers were at her blouse—that cheap, unlovely blouse that should never have sullied her honeyed-body—peeling the material away from her, careless of buttons just as he was careless of zips or fasteners, only to ease her skirt from her, let it slide and cascade to the floor, where he could lift her out of it and lower her gently, carefully, down upon the waiting bed.

He followed her in a daze, his own garments and her remaining ones shed somehow, anyhow. Irrelevant how they fell, or where. All that was essential was to lower his bared body onto hers, gleaming like pearl in the velvet dark, to graze his lips along that opalescent skin, the delicate bones below her throat, the hollow at its base. Then, with the lightest, most feathered touch, he skimmed the swell of her tender breasts, heard her murmurous cries, felt her breasts swelling to his touch of lips and fingertips, felt their peaks cresting beneath his sensuous suckling, heard those cries again, husky from her throat.

Her fingers wound in his hair, splaying out over the contours of his back, and his body hardened against hers, filling him with a desire so steep, so absolute, that he moved on her, seeking, questing, parting her thighs with his and lifting himself to her arching hips. Her throat was extended, her head thrown back, the pale tresses of her loosened hair flowing like a banner as he kissed her again, deeper and yet deeper still, as she opened to him with tiny, breathy cries, pleading for him as he slowly, carefully, sheathed himself within her yielding body.

She could not move. Dared not. Because if she did something impossible would happen. She would feel a bliss more than it was possible to feel. So she could only lie there, his body filling hers, hers enwrapping his, their muscles quivering. Her hands were caught at the wrists, lifted either side of her head. Her whole being was poised, balanced so finely that it was as if the very edge of a tsunami had welled out of the ocean deeps. For a timeless, exquisite moment she was held so still it was as if she were a statue of marble or ivory, hung in a moment of time that seemed eternal. She gazed upwards, her eyes wide, her lips parted—up into the face above her, whose dark, dark eyes held a question that was impossible to deny.

Then, with a susurration of her name, he moved.

And her body answered him.

She cried out. She could not help it—could not stop herself. Cried out as the drowning sweetness flushed through her until every cell was honeyed, every pore dissolved, and her whole body was drenched. The sweetness went on and on and on. He was there too, his body surging into her, and she heard him cry out with her. And then it was ebbing—ebbing away. The sweetness drained from her until all that was left was the utter exhaustion of her limbs, only lassitude. His body was heavy on hers, and he rolled them sideways so that she was in his arms, and he in hers, their bodies still melded, still complete. Her eyelids were so very, very heavy, her body sweet and warm. She folded against him, clasped to him, her hair swathing him, her head against his shoulder. Her breathing slowed, her heartbeat slowed, her eyelids fluttered shut and soon she was still, sleeping in his embrace.

Dim light pressed with skimming fingertips against her eyelids, fluttering them open. For a moment she was alone, as she had been for so long, and then, as if in a mirage, she realised she was in Nikos's arms.

And they had made love.

Happiness welled through her. How it had happened she did not care—nor why. It had happened, that was all, and she was here, and he was with her. Her hands could press against the warm, hard wall of his chest, feel the rise and fall of it, feel the soft rhythm of his breath. She could open her eyes and see, in the dim dawn light, the beautiful contours of his face, his sable hair feathering on his brow, his long, long lashes swept down over his eyes.

And know, with a wonder that was like a piercing pain, that she was experiencing something that she had never, ever experienced in her life.

I never lay in his arms, I never woke in his arms.

But this time—this time that had been granted to her!

This is how it should have been—

Her mind tried to sheer away, to block out the terrible memories that suddenly, instantly, were there inside her head, vivid and anguished. Humiliating and poisonous.

Shaming.

Cold iced through her. The warmth of Nikos's arms was gone. Blindly she stared out into the room.

And slowly, very, very slowly, as if a terrible, unbearable weight was crushing down on her, she knew what she must do.

CHAPTER EIGHT

'YOU do realise there's a recession, don't you?'

The voice of the woman in the Job Centre was sharp, impatient. Sophie knew why. She'd walked out of a perfectly good job, for no reason the woman could see—a jaunt to the countryside hardly counted—and now she was back again, wanting another job just like that.

'I'm willing to take anything,' Sophie said, her voice low.

Anxiety pressed at her. Although the cheque from Nikos was buying her blessed time, she had to start earning again as soon as she possibly could.

But she should not have thought of that cheque.

Nor of Nikos.

Like a guillotine, her mind slammed shut. A steel door rammed down across her memory. It took every ounce of her strength to hold it in place.

Focus—that's all you have to do! Focus on the only thing that matters now: getting another job. Any job.

The woman at the Job Centre was scrolling down her computer screen. 'There really is very little,' she said, disapproval still emanating from her. 'If you could type it might be different, but as it is you have no marketable skills.'

Sophie knew. Had known it for four bitter years. No marketable skills, and no time to acquire any. No time to do anything other than work all the hours she could, for whatever wages she could.

The woman sat back, defeated. 'You'll have to come in tomorrow. There may be more then. All that's on the database is casual bar work, and you said you didn't want that.'

No, Sophie didn't want that. She'd tried it once and found the inevitable sexual harassment repellent. Since then she'd stuck to shop work, which could run on into the evenings. But now she knew she had no leg to stand on in being picky about bar work. Not after she'd been prepared to work as an escort...

Even if *she* had denied the true nature of the work *Nikos had been right.*

But she couldn't think of Nikos. Absolutely, totally must not think of him. She looked across at the woman. Her expression was bleak.

'What's going in bar work?'

Ten minutes later she walked out on to the street. The dust and fumes of London hit her, worse than ever now, after the respite she'd had in the countryside. But that was the least of her problems. The biggest one was what it always had been—money. Even if she got the job she'd been sent to start that evening the money would be lousy. The basic hourly rate was grim. She ran sums in her head and felt fear bite.

Bleakly she trudged along the pavement. Her muscles still ached from the miles she'd walked yesterday. Down the long drive of the house at five in the morning, then a good two miles along the main road until she'd finally come to a village, found someone up and about at that early hour, and asked where the nearest train station was. It had turned out to be a taxi-ride away—a fare she could scarcely afford, let alone the price of a train ticket back to London. And she'd left her pitiful luggage behind her too. She had bolted with nothing more than her handbag, wearing the same clothes she had the night before because they'd been the only ones she could silently scrabble for as she edged from the bedroom, terrified Nikos would wake. Terrified her nerve would crack and she would be unable to do what she had to do…

But I did it, and that's all that matters! Nothing else—nothing else…

Despair crowded into her mind. She tried to fight it off, but it settled like a grey, chill miasma over her.

I have to keep going. That's all I must think about. Keep going.

And above all I must not think about what happened with Nikos! Because if I do…if I do…

Dear God, if she let herself think, remember, feel anything about what had happened, she would collapse, sit down on the kerb and weep, until her body was wrung out and she was simply dust on the street to be blown away into oblivion.

It was an aberration, a dream—that's all. That's how I have to think of it. As if I'd dreamt it. Because that's all it was. A dream. As unreal as if I had imagined it. As impossible as if I had imagined it.

But, try as she did to tell herself that, it seemed her body knew better. Her body was crying out to her that that extraordinary, miraculous night, that gift that had been given to her out of nowhere, *had* been real.

She could remember with every cell just how exquisite his every caress had been, every touch of his lips, every beautiful, incredible sensation he had aroused in her as he had made love to her slowly, sensuously, tenderly, passionately…

She stumbled on, forcing herself to do so. Finding words

in her head that she did not want there—could not allow there. But they came all the same, just as the echoes of his caresses trembled in her limbs, set an aching in her breasts, her heart. Her stricken, broken heart.

How can a heart break twice?

Hadn't it been agony enough to go through it the first time around, without having to endure it again now? Yet she knew that there was no escape—could be no escape. Nikos had come back into her life, and her heart had broken all over again.

It was that simple, that brutal.

If only he'd never seen me again!

And yet…

How could she wish never to have seen Nikos again? Never to have experienced that miraculous, magical night she had spent with him? It had been a blessing she could never regret! Emotion poured through her. Whatever the reason Nikos had taken her she must be glad—glad with all her heart—that he had! Because this time her abiding memory would not be burning humiliation and coruscating shame, tearing her to pieces, but instead something she could treasure all her life— a precious gift to hoard and protect, not reject with loathing and repulsion and anger.

That's what I must hold on to! To give me the strength to go on.

For go on she must—there was no alternative. There never had been.

Head bowed, she went on walking the hard pavement.

'Sir, we've got a sighting.'

Instantly Nikos tensed, fingers gripping his mobile. 'Where?' he barked.

His security operative gave him the location. Nikos

scrawled it on a pad, then cleared the line, before punching through to his chauffeur to order his car to the forecourt and relaying the location for him to key into the car's satnav. Then, striding from the office, pausing only to instruct his PA to cancel all appointments, he swung out into the corridor of the executive suite of Kazandros Corp's London headquarters and headed for the lift. His expression was grim.

His mood grimmer.

Finally his quarry had been run to earth. Emotion scythed through him, but he cut it short. For twenty-four hours emotion had rampaged through him, all but stopping him from functioning. Consuming him to the exclusion of everything else. From the moment he had finally realised that Sophie had gone—disappeared—not just from his bed, but from Belledon itself.

It had taken him over an hour of increasingly frantic searching through the near-derelict main house to establish that she was not lying with a broken neck at the foot of collapsing stairs, or fallen through the rotten floorboards. Even longer to realise that, despite having left all her belongings behind, unpacked, she had nevertheless gone—left him.

Why? The question still burned at the base of his mind, though he had stopped trying to find an answer. There was none that he could think of. It was inexplicable—unforgivable.

What the hell was she playing at?

Anger bit in his throat and he thrust it away. As he climbed into the car, throwing himself back in his seat and ordering his chauffeur, 'Just drive!', his face took on a closed, brooding expression. He'd been a fool. A total fool.

Just like last time.

Sophie Granton had torn him to shreds all over again. The burning in the pit of his stomach intensified, and so did the grim expression on his drawn features. He would find Sophie—find her, shake her like a rag, and get answers!

Damn her—damn her for doing this to me all over again! Taking me to heaven—then tossing me into hell. Damn her!

The drive to the location he'd been given took longer than he'd expected. From the plush Kazandros offices in the City the car wended its way north-west—but not to any of the prosperous areas of London that he would once have associated with Sophie Granton. But then these days Sophie Granton was no longer a Holland Park princess. As the car headed into more downmarket streets, Nikos glanced out through the smoked-glass windows, frowning. This area was not just downmarket, it was derelict!

His mobile sounded again, and he snapped it open.

'Yes?' His voice was curt.

'The subject is now walking along the street designated as her home address,' came the voice at the other end of the connection.

'Just keep her under surveillance,' said Nikos, before relaying the information to his driver.

His frown darkened as he looked about him. Then he saw her. She was some way ahead of the car, trudging along the pavement. There was something about the way she was walking that stung in his memory. He'd seen her walking like that once before, her head bowed, only just managing to put one foot in front of another. It had been the night he'd set eyes on her trudging through the rain in her tawdry finery, escaping from Cosmo Dimistris.

Defeated. Exhausted. Broken.

For a split second emotion knifed in him like a blade in his heart, twisting it painfully. Then a more predominant emotion surged again.

'Stop the car!'

The chauffeur did not need telling twice. He slowed to a halt and Nikos leapt from the car, striding along the pavement, past pedestrians, with a heavy, rapid tread. She was right ahead of him.

He clamped his hand on her shoulder and spun her round. She gave half a cry, her face suddenly shot with terror. Then she saw who it was.

She went white.

'Nikos.' Her voice was a breath, her skin taut over her cheekbones.

'Yes, *Nikos*!' he snarled. 'And now you can tell me what the *hell* you think you're playing at!'

Her expression blanked—completely blanked. For a second Nikos felt fury shoot through him, and then he realised that she was not deliberately blanking him, not deigning to shut him out. She was blank because she couldn't answer him. It was the same beaten, broken look she had had when he'd scooped her up, soaking wet, off the street.

The pressure of his hand on her shoulder slackened. He had to talk to her, get answers. But not here—not on the street.

'Where do you live, Sophie?' His eyes glanced around—surely she didn't live here? It might not be officially a slum, but the whole place was seedy and malodorous, with litter in the street, and graffiti, and clearly vandalised buildings.

She pointed vaguely to a building a few metres away. The lower storey was a boarded-up shop, and at the side was a door, inset with chipped and peeling paint.

'You live *there*?' The shock in Nikos's voice was open. *What the hell is going on? Why is she reduced to this total dump?*

Well, he would get answers to that, too. He would get all the answers he needed.

The car had drawn up alongside him now. It was drawing attention—it was not the kind of car that frequented an area like this. He crossed briefly to the driver and spoke to him, telling him to cruise around the block until he was called back. The car glided off, and Nikos turned his attention to Sophie. His hand was still on her shoulder.

He thought he could feel her trembling.

He walked her to the door she'd indicated, and waited while she fumblingly got out the keys and opened it. Inside, a smell of dirt, decay and stale urine hit him. There was no hallway, just a flight of stairs going straight up. At the top were several doors.

'This one,' said Sophie in a low voice, and opened it.

There was a single room beyond, and as he stepped inside Nikos realised that whatever had happened to Sophie Granton since he had severed all contact four years ago it had not been good. The room was some kind of bedsit, with half the space occupied by a narrow bed, and opposite, in an alcove flanked by a built-in cupboard, a sink, with a small fridge to one side, topped by a miniature cooker sporting a pair of cooking rings on which were stacked two saucepans. A small kettle was on the draining board, plugged into a loose socket on the wall. The floor covering was cracked vinyl, with a tiny rug beside the bed, and the curtains were faded around the window, which looked down into a cramped yard at the back of the house. The sole virtue of the room was that it was clean, tidy, and smelled of disinfectant.

'You live here—'

It was neither a question nor a statement. It was a voicing of disbelief.

She had put her bag down on the bed. 'Yes,' she said.

She seemed very calm, but her face and eyes were still blank.

He looked at her a moment. She was not meeting his eyes; she didn't seem to be able to. He paused a moment, then spoke.

'What in God's name is going on?' He took a breath, sharp and scissored. 'How can you live in this hole?'

She blinked, as if the question were a strange one. 'It's all I can afford.'

He said something in Greek, sibilant and angry.

'*Why?* Sophie, your father was a millionaire several times over! Even losing his business can't have reduced him to this! He will have put money aside, ring-fenced it. Even if it wasn't a fortune, like he had before, he would hardly end up a pauper! So why the hell are you living like this?'

His eyes narrowed suddenly. 'Have you fallen out with him?' Speculation laced his expression. 'Does he disapprove of your lifestyle? Is that it? Was that really the first time you'd worked as an escort, or were you feeding me a line?' A new thought struck him, cold, and horrible. 'Are you doing drugs, Sophie?'

He studied her. It had never crossed his mind that she might be, but now, looking at her, he wondered. When he'd held her in his arms he'd thought her wand-slim—was her slenderness the shedding of flesh that drugs could cause? Just as they could cause penury and desperation—enough to make her risk working as an escort?

Did she tell me she was paying off credit-card debts, or was that just my assumption? Was she really paying for drugs?

The shake of her head was infinitesimal, but it was there all the same, and Nikos found relief snaking through him. Then incomprehension took over again. So why *was* she living like this?

'Does your father know this is where you live?'

The question seemed to send a jolt through her, and emotion jagged in her eyes for a second. There was another imperceptible shake of her head. She wrapped her arms around herself, as if she were bandaging her body. As if she were wounded.

Something was wrong, Nikos knew, with foreboding. Very wrong.

'Why haven't you told your father, Sophie?' His voice was low. 'He couldn't possibly want you to live here! He would help you get on your feet—you know he would! Maybe you feel you should be independent at your age, not rely on him financially, but—'

A sound broke from her. It might have been a laugh, but Nikos knew it was not. She looked at him. Straight at him.

'He hasn't got any money,' she said. Her arms seemed to tighten around her, and the wildness in her eyes intensified. She was under huge emotional stress, Nikos could see, and he knew he had to tread very, very carefully or she would break into pieces.

He looked at her. 'I don't understand,' he said carefully.

This time she did laugh. But it was hollow and wild. 'Don't you? Tell me, Nikos, you who operate up in the financial stratosphere, does *your* fiscal expertise go downmarket at all? Do *you*, running a company the size of Kazandros, ever come across any slang jargon in the financial field? Does the term "boiler room" mean anything to you?' Her voice was cruel, and vicious. But again it was not him she was aiming at.

He stilled. 'Yes,' he said.

Boiler room—slang for financial operations so fraudulent the financial authorities were forever struggling to combat them. Like fetid mushrooms, as soon as one was closed down another sprang up to take its place. Shady in the extreme, and highly, obscenely profitable for those who ran them. Always hungry for more and yet more investors, persuading them by slick, sophisticated marketing to invest in worthless bogus shares and then, when the promised returns did not material-ise, persuading them to invest more and yet more to recoup their original investment, to get to the magic pot of gold at the end of the shoddy rainbow.

Until they had no more money left to invest. Until they had been bled dry. And then the scam merchants moved on to the next victim.

Nikos's brows drew together in puzzlement. Surely Edward Granton, a long-term, big-league corporate player, would have recognised a boiler-room scam? Known not to go near it? So how the hell had he got trapped in its fraudulent coils?

He pushed the question aside. Right now it wasn't impor-tant. Right now only one thing was important. His gaze swept condemningly around the dingy bedsit. Revulsion rose in him. He took her elbow.

'We're getting out of here,' he said.

Her eyes flared suddenly, and then, like a shadow falling, they went blank again.

'You go, Nikos,' she said, in that low, dead voice.

He gave a brief, rasping laugh. 'There is no way on earth, Sophie, that I am leaving you in this dump. Get your things—we're going.' He glanced around again at the bare room. 'There can't be much here, and anyway—' his voice tightened '—I have the things you left at Belledon.'

'I…I'll come and collect them,' she said falteringly.

'They're only fit for the trash,' he riposted.

'They're all I've got. Please.' Her voice sounded anxious. 'Please let me collect them—don't throw them away. I need them. And,' she went on, forcing herself, 'I'm fine here—honestly. I'm used to it.'

She took another razoring breath. She needed him to go. Just go. She was starting to break, and she mustn't break in front of him—she just mustn't. The stark shock of his approach on the street was wearing off, leaving in its place only an urgency to get rid of him. She *had* to get rid of him. She had to. It had taken all the strength she possessed to leave him that fateful morning, to force herself to walk away, down the long, long road back to the bleak, hopeless life to which she was condemned and from which there could be no escape.

And now to see him again, to have him here, so close, in this vile dump she lived in, was agony—just agony!

'Please go, Nikos. I can't have you here. I just can't.' Her voice was strained. 'I've… I've got things I have to do. So, please—just go. Please.'

'What things?' He was unrelenting.

'Just things. It doesn't matter what. Just go, please.'

He could see her distress. It was visible, flaring from her. And he could see, too, that she was at the very end of her strength. She could take no more. And he needed to find out a lot more! His eyes set on Sophie as she stood there, looking so frail a breath of wind might blow her away.

'Where is your father, Sophie?' The question came stark, blunt.

He saw her cheeks whiten. He was stressing her, but right now he didn't care—he had to know where Edward Granton was, and then go and confront him with the truth about his daughter, his once-precious daughter!

What father would leave his daughter to live like this?

'He's abroad,' she answered quickly.

'Where?'

She gave a shrug, a small, weakened movement, her eyes shifting from his relentless gaze. 'It doesn't matter where. Nikos. Look, you have to go,' Her voice was taut, low. 'I…I have to be somewhere.'

Nikos levelled a long, measuring look on her. She did not meet his eyes. They were blank, blind, her expression a mask. A mask to hide behind. While behind the mask she was falling to pieces…

He took a step back, nodding. 'OK—I'll go.'

He saw the tension in her face ebb by a fraction, and knew he was doing the right thing. His agenda had just changed. The reasons why she had walked out on him could wait—for now. For one long, last moment he looked at her. Then, with a final brief nod of his head, he turned on his heel and left.

She listened as his footsteps rang on the stairs, heard the door to the street open and shut. Then slowly, very slowly, she sank down on the bed, as tears welled up under her eyelids and burnt like acid on her skin.

CHAPTER NINE

OUT on the pavement, Nikos slid out his mobile phone. Although he could not see his operative—they were skilled at inconspicuous surveillance—he knew the man was in the vicinity. When he answered, Nikos's instructions were quick and to the point.

'Keep watching her.' Then he disconnected and called his driver to bring the car for him.

His mood was savage. But not with Sophie. Not know.

What the hell was going on with her? Why was her father leaving her to live such a life? Running up debts! Taking menial jobs! Queuing up at Job Centres! Resorting to working as an escort!

Everything he'd thought he'd known about her life now had exploded in his face.

But he would find out the truth! The truth about why she had run from him, walked out on him as she had, after such a night together…

No time to think of that now. No time to do anything other than ruthlessly, relentlessly, do whatever it took to keep her in his sights.

His car pulled up at the kerb and he stepped into it, curtly ordered his driver to drive off. Sophie had to think he had, indeed, done as she had pleaded with him to do—left her alone.

A thin, whipped smile set at his lips. One thing was certain—Sophie Granton was not getting away from him. Wherever she was going now, he'd be there too.

His car meandered through the nearby streets, and it did not take long before the call came through from his street sur-veillance team that Sophie had left the dump she lived in. But when Nikos arrived at the destination she had made for, in an outer region of London, whose quiet, wide, tree-lined avenues and large Victorian villas were a world away from the litter-strewn, run-down area she lived in, he could only frown in consternation. It was a substantial edifice, with a brass plate discreetly set into the stone wall fronting the short driveway past the entrance.

What was she doing here? At such a place? For a moment he could only stare, beyond comprehension. Then logic clicked in. The only explanation was that this place was some-thing to do with her earlier visit to the Job Centre. She must be here for some kind of job interview—what else? Climbing out of the car pulled up in the driveway, he walked inside.

'I'm looking for Sophie Granton,' he announced to the re-ceptionist at the desk, volunteering no other information. The young woman looked momentarily flustered, a female re-action Nikos was familiar with, but she glanced down at the arrivals list and nodded.

'She's just arrived,' she acknowledged. 'I'm sure it will be fine for you to go through,' she told him flutteringly. 'It's such a lovely day everyone is out in the garden. If you turn to the right you'll see a door leading directly into the grounds.'

Well, perhaps, thought Nikos, striding off, in a place like this it made sense to conduct job interviews outdoors. He looked around him, his expression grim. However necessary such places were, they could hardly be cheerful places to work, in any capacity. Physical strength was probably a necessity too, he surmised, and Sophie hardly fitted the bill on that. She had looked as fragile as bone china when she'd stood in that slum she had to call home. His expression grew grimmer. The discovery of just how poverty-stricken her circumstances were had shocked him—the reason for them even more so.

Discomforting thoughts crowded his mind. Thoughts he did not want to think. About everything that had happened to her since he had thrown her from him that fatal night four years ago.

He reached the door the receptionist had indicated and stepped through. Beyond was a paved area with a lawn. It was secluded, but spacious, bordered by flowerbeds and ornamental shrubs, all very manicured. It must cost money to be here. Yet, however good the amenities, it was not a place one could ever want to spend time. How could it be?

He scanned the garden, looking past the occupants with a sombre countenance. Then, at the far side of the lawn, standing beside a wooden bench, he saw her. He arrowed his gait, making straight for his target, ignoring everything else but her. She did not see him coming, was absorbed in her conversation— her interview?—with a woman who was clearly a member of staff. Then the woman nodded and turned away, heading in a different direction, and in that instant Sophie saw him.

She could feel herself going faint. She must be hallucinating. It could not be—*could not be!*—Nikos, striding across the lawn towards her. What was he *doing* here?

How had he even known where she was going? She hadn't

thought she was likely to be able to get here today, but because the Job Centre had only been able to steer her towards evening work, she had seized the unexpected opportunity to come.

Nikos must have followed her here—it was the only explanation.

But why? Why would he do such a thing? For what purpose? Surely he'd said everything he'd wanted to say already—or else why leave her the way he had when she'd asked him to go? Nikos Kazandros was not a man who obeyed orders unless he wanted to.

Numbly, she faced him as he came up to her.

'Job interview over?' His enquiry was civil, but his eyes were veiled, as if he had spoken merely to mask his true question.

She looked at him blankly, unable to answer. Her mind was reeling.

I can't take any more of this—I just can't.

Mental and emotional exhaustion numbed her. His eyes were boring into her, like nails. She wanted to shut her eyes, shut him out, but she couldn't. Why was he persecuting her like this? *Why?*

'Nikos…' Her voice was like a thread. 'I can't take any more.' Her words were an echo of her thoughts. 'I can't.'

She wanted to blink him out of existence, because it was unbearable that he should be here.

He ignored her words. His eyes only flicked briefly around, taking in the scene, his expression controlled. 'You are seriously considering working here?' he put to her.

She opened her mouth to answer, but stayed her voice. Her head turned instead. Nikos followed her line of sight. Someone was approaching. As they came near, he could feel the blood drain from his face.

Thee mou—

The recognition was instant—the shock like a shot to his lungs.

Sophie was going forward, greeting the arrival. Her voice was soft, emotion trembling in it. 'Hello, Dad,' she said.

As if frozen, Nikos watched the hunched figure in the wheelchair being steered by a nurse. He raised his sunken head with visible difficulty, his gaze seeking Sophie with hazy effort. She went forward and stooped to kiss him tenderly on his cheek.

'I got the afternoon off,' she said to him, with the same soft, tender note in her voice, 'so I've come to see you. How are you today?'

It was the nurse who answered—the same woman Nikos had seen talking to Sophie a moment earlier.

'All the better for seeing you—isn't that right?' She addressed her patient for corroboration, and Nikos watched him making a slow nod. A word came from his lips, low, and enunciated with obvious difficulty.

'Sophie.'

It was a single word, but there was a lifetime of love in it.

Nikos felt the cords of his throat contract, and could only stand, motionless, while Sophie sat herself down on the bench, the wheelchair positioned right beside it, so she could take the inert hand lying on her father's lap.

The nurse glanced at Nikos. 'You've got an extra visitor today, Mr Granton,' she said. Her voice had a note of professional, determined cheerfulness in it. Nikos knew why. Anyone whose task it was to care for patients in such a condition had to be relentlessly upbeat—or they would be unable to carry on.

The drooping eyes lifted with difficulty again. Nikos felt his shoulders stiffen. 'It's good to see you again,' he said. It was a lie, but he managed it.

It was *not* good to see Edward Granton again—not like this. It was not good to see a man obviously stricken with a catastrophic blow, confined to a wheelchair, barely able to speak, reduced to a hollow shell.

There was no recognition in the drooping eyes, and Nikos could see puzzlement, as though Edward Granton were searching painfully for who he was. But Nikos was reluctant to give his name—the last thing he wanted right now was for the man he'd left to face financial ruin to remember who he was. He could feel his stomach knotting, as if he'd swallowed a stone.

Edward Granton's troubled gaze slipped to his daughter's, and Nikos could see the softening in his expression as she squeezed his hand reassuringly.

'It's all right, Daddy,' she said, and the use of the childish diminutive made the stone feel harder still in Nikos's stomach. Memory pierced through him—Sophie calling Edward Granton 'Daddy' had half amused him, half made him realise just how very young she was, despite her years. A bleak look flashed in his eyes. Well, Sophie Granton was old beyond her years now.

Thee mou—what had happened? What had happened to reduce Edward Granton to this?

Sophie was talking to her father, murmuring to him, leaning forward, still holding his hand in hers, shutting out the world. Nikos glanced at the nurse.

He spoke to her, keeping his voice low. 'Can you tell me what caused his condition?'

'Stroke,' said the nurse, her voice low and professionally concerned. 'He's doing very well, considering. It was very nearly fatal, and of course it came on top of all his other health problems. Two heart attacks took their toll, and weakened him considerably. When the stroke hit he wasn't expected to survive, but his daughter has been an absolute tower of strength, and has performed wonders to pull him through. He's still extremely frail, as you can see, but so much better than he was at the beginning.'

Nikos swallowed. 'How…how long since he had his stroke?'

'Well over a year now,' answered the nurse. 'Of course it's excellent that he was able to come here when he was released from hospital. If I say so myself this is a first-class clinic for stroke rehabilitation—and I believe it's made a significant difference to his prognosis. Which is why,' she ran on confidingly, 'it would be disastrous if he had to leave.'

'Leave?'

'Well,' the nurse went on—and Nikos was pretty sure it was because she enjoyed talking to him, as so many females did, and took ruthless advantage—'unfortunately the clinic is privately run, and it's understandable that a prolonged stay is sadly beyond the means of many people. But I would very, very much hope that it will be possible for him to continue here.'

Nikos could see her eyes going openly to take in his affluent appearance—the bespoke suit, the handmade shoes, the air of sleek prosperity. But his mind was elsewhere.

Not here. Not in this garden, where patients in wheelchairs were being perambulated by nurses or walking haltingly around, but in a taxi, with rain pounding on the windscreen and roof, and Sophie Granton's drowned face, cheekbones stark, eyes wild and vicious, mascara running down her hollowed cheeks, hissing at him, *'I need the bloody money…'*

Like in some dark, damnable game, the last of the pieces fell into place.

Gutting him.

He felt himself hollowing out as realisation kicked through him. Everything made sense now—and the sense it made shook him to the foundation. His eyes went to Sophie. So fragile-looking, yet she had had to bear a weight that would have broken anyone, let alone a girl brought up in wealthy comfort by an indulgent, protective, cosseting father who'd sheltered her from every financial chill. Yet both her doting father and her financial security had been ripped from her, leaving her to fend for herself and more—to take on the emotionally and financially crushing burden of care for a father reduced to a stricken figure in a wheelchair.

How had she done it?

The question sounded in Nikos's head, but he knew the answer already. She'd done what she'd had to.

Whatever it had taken. Giving up her music. Living in a slum. Working at one dead-end job after another. Working as an escort…

His mind sheered away, but he forced it back. *That* was why she'd taken that repellent job. His gaze moved around, to the manicured gardens and plentiful nurses and the well-kept clinic. He knew how much a place like this would cost.

And I thought she'd run up credit-card debts and didn't want to let her father know…

Anger at his own presumption stabbed at him. More than anger. For a moment his gaze came back to Sophie, who was still attending to her father, holding his hand, chatting to him tenderly, even though it was clear that Edward Granton found it painfully effortful to respond. They were absorbed in each other. Nikos let them be, and instead returned his attention to the nurse.

'Excuse me a moment,' he said, and headed back to the garden entrance to the clinic.

His business at the reception desk did not take long, and then he went out to the forecourt, where his car was waiting for him. He got in and went on waiting, busying himself with his laptop and some documents to pass the time, though his mind was seething with emotion that made concentrating on something as tedious as business all but impossible.

It was well over an hour before Sophie emerged from the clinic, looking drawn and pale. Nikos intercepted her immediately, allowing her no chance to do anything other than be steered peremptorily into the car.

She attempted to remonstrate. 'Nikos—what are you doing? I don't want—'

He cut her short. 'I need to talk to you.'

Her face closed. 'Well, I don't need to talk to *you*,' she retaliated, pulling away as far as possible along the wide back seat of the spacious interior of the car, with its glass panelling to keep occupants private from the driver.

She was bristling with hostility, he could see, and rounded on him like a cornered animal.

'What is this, Nikos? What the hell are you following me for? What's it to do with you what I do with my life?'

He looked at her. A long, level look. 'You ask *me* that?'

It was all he said, but it was all he needed to say. For a moment their eyes locked, and in them was an infinity of memory.

'Nikos—' Her breath was a sigh, her mouth warm and soft and so, so generous beneath his. He could not resist kissing her. Could not resist folding her against him, feeling the swell of her tender breasts against him, the slender curve of her body wrapped in his arms. Feel, too, the response of his body to her closeness...

He sought to draw away. This was impossible! A torment beyond enduring! Already he had gone far, far further than he'd intended. But, again, he'd been unable to resist. They had been out for the evening, a charity dinner-dance, and she was looking so beautiful he'd thought he would never be able to take his eyes from her. And when he had driven her home she had persuaded him—fool that he was, and tempted beyond reason!—to come in for coffee. And here, now, on the plush sofa in the low-lit drawing room of her father's house, he had taken her in his arms, unable to resist...

But resist he must! She had already artlessly let slip that her father was away on business, and Nikos knew that he had flown up to Edinburgh that day to see if another source of rescue package for his company could be put together, even at this late hour. And so it was dangerous beyond all things for him to be here, alone in the house with her. But he was on fire for her! And despite all his resolutions that he must not do what every cell in his body was urging him to do, still he did not leave— did not get to his feet, remind her that his flight to Athens was early the next morning, that he must get back to his hotel.

She was clinging to him, her mouth open to his, her fingers winding into his hair, sliding around the column of his waist, and he could recognise, with the experience of his years, that she was becoming as aroused as he was. And it was madness to let it happen! Madness!

And yet insanity possessed him—overtook him. He let her draw him to his feet, let her take his hand, her eyes glowing, ardent, let her lead him from the room, ascend the stairs to her bedroom. He tried—he truly tried to resist as she embraced him again.

'Sophie—I mustn't—I must go—'

But she was oblivious, feverish with mounting desire, as beyond reason as he was—he could tell. And he gloried in it, rejoiced in it—that she should be as ardent, as inflamed for him as he was for her. But one of them had to stay sane...surely one of them must?

'Nikos—oh, Nikos!' Her very voice enticed him, entreated him! 'Don't go—please, don't go—please—'

How could he resist? How? When she was pleading for the very thing he wanted more than anything else in the world?

So he let insanity possess him.

And then afterwards he paid the price. A price he had never thought he would have to pay.

She was lying in his arms, her body curled against his, her hair like a silken scarf around him, her hectic heart rate slowing now, as was his, as he lay consumed by wonder, murmuring endearments to her, tender and loving, possessed by such emotion as he had not known existed. She was everything that he had dreamed of! He could not regret what had happened! How could he? It had been a voyage to a paradise he had never known before—a destination that he knew now, with absolute certainty, would be his home for ever.

Her eyes were shining with joy, and emotion kicked through him again just to see it.

'Oh, Nikos! Darling, darling Nikos! I'm so, so happy—so blissfully, blissfully happy! I can't believe it really happened— I can't believe that it's all right. It's just like a fairy tale!'

She kissed him, her eyes like jewels.

'We can be married now, can't we? And everything's going to be so wonderful! You and me together! For ever and ever! Bliss, bliss, bliss! And Daddy will be all right too, because I know you'll save his company and everything will be fine again.'

He stilled. He could feel it happening.

'What did you just say?'

She gazed at him, eyes veiling suddenly. 'I'm sorry! Oh, I'm sorry, Nikos! I shouldn't have said that, I know. But I've been worried about him, and now I'm just so relieved I don't have to worry about him after all, and—'

He did not let her finish. Sharply he pulled away. Out of her clinging embrace. He threw back the bedcovers and stood up. Looked down at her. Looked down at the beautiful, pale, slender body he had just possessed.

And knew the price he was expected to pay for it.

'Nikos?' Her voice was uncertain again, and he could hear the note of anxiety in it. Well, she was right to be anxious. Her prey was about to escape her. Coolly, methodically, he started to get dressed. But inside he felt a hot, raging maelstrom of emotion boiling in him.

'Nikos?' Her tremulous query came. 'Where—where are you going?'

'Where?' His riposte was cool. As cool as the manner in which he was swiftly doing up his dress shirt, fastening his cuffs. 'Back to my hotel, of course.' His eyes were veiled in the dim light, but he could see her body in all its beauty, all its lost innocence, in a soft pool of lamplight. Emotion boiled in him again, but he would not let it show. He reached for his dinner jacket, abandoned on a chair in their haste to undress each other only a short while ago, shrugging it on across his broad shoulders.

'Did you really think I would bail out Granton on your account? That I would save your father's company just for a taste of your body? That offering up your virginity would get me to marry you and I would then rescue your father and keep you a rich man's daughter?'

He stood looking down at her, and everything he felt about her—knew about her—was in the obliterating knifing of his eyes. His voice, when he spoke, cut like a whip. Harsh. Condemning. Contemptuous.

'You had it all planned, didn't you? All along.' He paused. 'What a contemptible little piece of work you are.'

Then he turned and walked out of her bedroom. Every muscle in his body had to be forced.

He had scarcely gained the top of the stairs when she came hurtling after him.

'Nikos! No, please! Please!' She was clinging to him, naked, her voice terrified, sobbing. He put her from him, hands clamping around her bare upper arms like vices.

'Enough! The game is over, Sophie. Over.' He let go of her, and went on down the stairs. Right on down to the ground floor. The last he heard of her was her broken, hysterical sobbing. The crying of his name.

CHAPTER TEN

THE car drove on through the traffic, heading back into central London. Sophie had seemed to acquiesce, and was sitting on the far side of the seat still, but no longer protesting or vocal. Her eyes were closed, her face was shuttered, shutting him out. Tension and exhaustion were in every line of her body. Nikos let her be. This was not the place for what had to be done. Silently he resumed reading the document he'd been attempting to study while he'd waited for her to come out of the clinic. But the words were meaningless. Only one thing had meaning now, and that must wait until their journey's end.

It seemed to take for ever until his car finally pulled in under the portico of his Park Lane hotel and his driver was opening the door on Sophie's side. She got out, and Nikos was there instantly, lest she try and bolt. But she stood listless, immobile, as he cupped her elbow and steered her inside the hotel lobby. She remained silent until he had escorted her up in the elevator to his suite, and then, as he closed the door, she turned.

'We have nothing to say to each other, Nikos. Nothing!'

Her voice was neither hostile nor encouraging. It was indifferent. As if she had switched off somewhere along the journey.

'Sit down,' he instructed her, and with the same dumb acquiescence she lowered herself down onto the sofa.

He followed suit, but sat himself at the far end. He could see her tensing, but ignored it. He had his own tension to cope with. He had to stay in control of this conversation, and he needed all his self-control to do so.

'I want to know,' he spelt out, 'exactly what has happened since I walked out on you, Sophie, four years ago.'

She eyed him blankly. Her face was closed. 'Why?' The indifference was there still, but there was hostility beneath the surface now. He could tell.

He ignored the challenge. 'Just tell me.' He paused. 'You're going nowhere till we've had this conversation, so you'd better get on with it. What happened after I walked out on you four years ago?'

Her face was blank. Jaw set. OK, he would start jabbing. 'When did your father have his first heart attack?'

He'd got to her, he could see. She hadn't expected that. 'Who told you he'd had one?' she countered instantly, voice bristling.

'The nurse at the clinic. He had two before his stroke. So when was the first one?'

He could see the cords of her neck tauten. Then her head twisted back to him. 'It's not your damn business!'

Nikos ignored her outburst. 'When did he have his first heart attack, Sophie?'

'You want to know? OK, I'll tell you!' Her eyes were full of venom. 'He had his first heart attack the morning he flew back from Edinburgh, without a rescue package, when his PA told him you'd phoned to say there was no possibility of a Kazandros deal, either, and you'd flown back to Athens already.'

Nikos stilled. 'That morning?'

'You want to see his hospital records?' she jibed sarcastically.

But Nikos's mind was racing. *Thee mou,* the very next day after he'd thrown her from him like a soiled rag!

'How—how bad was he?'

'He pulled through,' she said tightly. 'The doctors warned me he might not, that he might have another attack, but he didn't. He was in hospital for months, and had to have surgery. That's why I dropped out of music college— to look after him. By then Granton had folded, and I was worried about university costing too much. The house in Holland Park had to go, too, and we moved to a much cheaper apartment.'

'I'm—sorry,' said Nikos. It seemed an inadequate thing to say.

She gave a half-shrug. 'Why? It wasn't anything to do with you. Not really. You weren't responsible—why should you have been?'

'Nevertheless,' he said stiffly. Emotion had started to slice inside him again, but he had to keep pushing. 'And the second attack?'

'A year later. That one was worse. He was a lot weaker. There was a lot more stress.'

'Stress?' Nikos pounced on the word.

She looked away again. 'Money things. He'd tried to start up Granton again. It stressed him. And then…' She paused a moment, then continued, in the same tight, terse manner. 'It was a drain on him financially, losing him even more money, and he had to pull the plug. That's what triggered the second heart attack.'

He nodded slowly. There was another question he had to ask to make the ugly, bleak jigsaw come together. 'You told me he'd got caught by a boiler-room scam. When did that happen?'

Had Edward Granton been so weakened by illness that he'd actually been stupid enough to fall for such a well-known fraud?

Sophie's eyes flared with emotion. He could not tell which one, but he knew it was one that caused pain. 'While he was back in hospital. I—I had power of attorney—he wasn't expected to pull through a second time—and I…I wanted to give Dad some good news, because he'd been so worried about money. So I… So I…'

Nikos felt icy cold go through him as realisation hollowed out in him.

'They targeted *you*, not your father.'

His mind reeled at the very thought of it. Sophie—sheltered by her father from every financial reality in life, insulated from all necessity, focussing only on her music, her studies, her carefree, happy life—lured into the bloodsucking grip of leeches in a boiler room. It would have been like throwing a puppy to wolves.

To be torn to pieces.

Rage speared in him. Rage that *anyone* should have done that to her!

She was sitting very still, her hands knotted together in her lap. She looked at Nikos. Her skin was stretched across her cheekbones. Her eyes empty now.

'I invested nearly everything he had left. It wasn't much by then—only a couple of hundred thousand out of everything he'd once had. I was desperate to recoup his losses, so I could go to him and tell him everything was all right again! Instead—' She fell silent again, but guilt and self-condemnation lacerated her face. 'I lost him everything—everything he'd managed to salvage when his company went bust,' she whispered. 'Everything. I was so incredibly, incredibly stupid. Gullible. I tried to hide it from Dad, but when he finally came out of hospital he found out and…and…' She took a razored breath. 'That's when he had his stroke.'

She started to lace and unlace her fingers. 'He was lucky. Not just that he survived, but that he was able to go to that clinic. It's one of the best in the country. And even luckier that his health insurance was still running.' She swallowed, and then went on, staring blindly down at the carpet, the skin stretched across her cheekbones. 'But it's run out now. He's used up all his allowance, what with all the hospitalisation and surgery and so on, as well as the stroke clinic. I was putting aside all the money I could, spending as little as possible on anything else, but I couldn't keep up with the payments. So…so…when they said he would have to leave I knew I had to do whatever it took to earn enough money.'

She lifted her head suddenly, staring right at Nikos. Her expression was hard, and he saw the same look in her eyes as she'd had in the taxi, when he'd hauled her out of the gutter.

'And if that meant working as an escort, then so what? I had to have the money! I *had* to! Keeping Dad in the clinic is all that matters! And after all—' her voice twisted '—it's not as if he'd *know* how I was earning the money!' Her eyes were like knives, slicing into Nikos. 'So that's why I did it! And that's why I grabbed your money, too! So now you know! And why the hell you want to I haven't the faintest idea! It's nothing to you, Nikos—nothing!'

For a moment, as she fell silent, her chest heaving with emotion, he said nothing. But then he spoke.

'You're wrong,' he said, and his voice was different but he didn't know how. 'It's everything to me.'

His eyes held hers—held them as if he were reaching for them from a very, very long way away. Across a divide that engulfed them like a bottomless chasm.

Emotion was huge inside him, overwhelming him in its enormity. But there were questions still to ask. Questions upon which his whole being depended.

'Why did you make love with me, Sophie? At Belledon?' His voice was low.

Her eyes flickered, as if she were seeking refuge.

'Why, Sophie?' he asked again, in the same low, intense voice.

Her face worked, but she would not answer. Her eyes slid away, unable to meet his.

'We found ecstasy together.' His voice was lower still. 'You cannot deny it—nor I. Ecstasy, Sophie, that night at Belledon.' He paused, and a world was in that pause. 'Then you left. Why, Sophie?'

Slowly, as if every word were dragged from her, as if she was forcing herself to speak, she answered him.

'I had to. I couldn't…I couldn't endure it all over again. Having you despise me.' Her face contorted. 'Hate me, just as you did four years ago! I couldn't face it—not again!' She shuddered. 'Not when this time I was innocent!' She looked at him, eyes stricken. 'But you wouldn't have believed me— and why should you have, after what I'd done to you? I swear to you, Nikos, I was innocent! But you already knew I was desperate for money, and if you'd found out about what had happened to my father you would simply have thought that I was as guilty now as I was four years ago!'

Her face contorted again, anguish and self-loathing in her eyes. 'Because four years ago I *was* guilty! Guilty of every word you threw at me! I'd just found out that day about my father's financial troubles—I saw an article in the business section of a newspaper someone was reading on the bus as I came back from college, headlined "Granton counts on

Kazandros lifeline"! I was horrified! Appalled! Terrified for
my father! And I felt so totally ashamed! I'd spent all that time
tunnel-visioned on you. I'd never even realised what was
going on for my father!'

She gave a hollow, biting laugh, quickly cut off in her
throat. 'Until I read in that article that that was why my father
had invited you in the first place! Because he wanted you to
be his white knight, to save him from going under! I felt so
guilty that my father was in such trouble and I hadn't even
noticed! But then I realized…' She swallowed. 'I realised that
of course you must be intending to invest in Grantons, or
merge, or whatever was going to be necessary, because you
would never have been going out with me if you hadn't! I
knew you would never have had a relationship with me if you
weren't intending to save Granton. You would have thought
it dishonourable, because your going out with me would have
led my father to assume he could count on you. So, because
you *were* still going out with me, I knew I *didn't* have to worry
about my father after all. And then that evening—'

She stopped. Her chest was heaving, and suddenly she got
to her feet.

'And then,' she went on, each word cutting the air, 'that
evening, at that charity ball, you told me you were going
back to Athens the next morning.'

She stopped again and swallowed. There was a stone in her
throat, and she had to swallow it. Nikos was sitting immobile,
looking at her. His face was a mask, and she knew why. She
forced herself on, each word like broken glass in her throat.

'I knew that could only mean one thing. You were finished
with me. And that meant you were finished with my father,
too. That you weren't going to be his white knight. And you
weren't going to be my—'

She took another razoring breath. The stone in her throat was still there, but she had to force herself to speak all the same. Why, she didn't know. Nikos knew the truth. He had known it four years ago. He knew it now.

'So it was to be our last evening together—ever. And I couldn't bear it. I couldn't bear it. So I invited you in, knowing we'd be alone in the house, and I made myself as…as enticing as I could. It…it was like…like a test. Were you *really* going to finish with me? Were you *really* going to leave me?' Her voice dropped. Her hands twisted in her lap, eyes sank.

'I so, so desperately wanted you to stay.'

Her words came haltingly, each one exacting a price from her in blood.

'And you did stay.' She lifted her eyes to him again. Forced herself to look at him. Face him. Confess to him. 'You stayed. And you made love to me. I knew you would never have done that if you hadn't been serious about me, about our relationship, because you knew I was a virgin, and I knew you would always respect that. So to me that night was proof that you hadn't been going to finish with me after all, that you were serious about me and always had been, and that you would sort out everything about the business side of things just as you must have intended all along! We'd get married and live happily ever after, and all Daddy's worries would be gone because you'd be his son-in-law, and you and your father would be investing in Granton, and Daddy would be happy, and you and I would be happy, and everything in the entire universe was going to be *wonderful*! Just *wonderful*! A fairy tale come true, with you as a white knight for my father and for me too!'

Her voice was rank with bitterness, with self-mockery. Self-loathing.

She looked at him. His face was still a motionless mask.

'And then…' She swallowed, and the stone was choking her now, suffocating her. 'Then you told me the truth. About myself. Threw those ugly, brutal home truths at me—showing me just what I'd done.'

Her eyes shut a moment, as if she did not have the strength to keep them open. Then she took another breath and spoke again.

'And I realised it was true—every word of what you'd said. I realised I'd behaved shamefully, trying to manipulate you, luring you into bed with me. You called me a contemptible little piece of work—and I was. I hated you for it, Nikos, but it was true.'

Her eyes burned in her face. 'But not this time…'

His face had shuttered, veiled as if by a mask. He sat back, leaning back against the sofa, spreading his arms along the cushions, crossing one leg over another. Elegant, devastating. In the pit of her churning stomach, Sophie felt a clench suddenly.

Get out! Get out while you can! You were mad to let him bring you here! You've said your piece—for what the hell it was worth!—now go!

She took a heavy, angry, heaving breath. He looked so damn relaxed, lounging back on the sofa! So damnably devastating! Greedily, hungrily, her eyes devoured him, even though she tried to stop herself. But this would be the very last time she would set eyes on him. In a moment she would be gone out of his life for ever. And never, never again would she see his face in the flesh, see the perfect curve of his cheekbones, the blade of his perfect nose, the sculpted, sensuous mouth that could make her run with hot and cold if she let herself, for a single second, remember the touch of his lips on her flesh, and the eyes, those beautiful, dark, gold-glinting, long-lashed eyes, that she could drown in, down, down, down into their depths, never to surface…

With all the strength she had left, she pulled herself to her feet. A raking breath left her stricken lungs. 'I'm going now, Nikos. There's nothing else you need to know.'

She made to turn, to head for the door of the suite, but his words stayed her in her tracks.

'You're wrong. There is something I need to know—very badly.'

His words seemed casual, as did his pose, but there was a fine tension in every line of his body that belied his calm.

'And there are things *you* need to know, Sophie.' He paused, as if imposing self-control for a moment. 'And the first is this. I've paid your father's clinic fees for the next six months.'

For a second she froze, then she rounded on him. 'Then you can damn well *un*pay them! I didn't ask for your help, Nikos! I didn't ask for your charity! My father's not your concern! Not your responsibility!'

He got to his feet, and suddenly he seemed very tall, his presence overpowering. She took a step backwards.

'You're wrong,' he said again, and walked towards her. 'Because there's something else you need to know, Sophie.' He stopped a few steps away from her, but it was like being in a magnetic field, and she felt herself physically sway. She dug her heels into the carpet, standing her ground, muscles knotted with tension.

'There's *nothing* else I need to know!'

He shook his head. 'You're wrong about that, too, Sophie. Wrong about so, so much. But mostly wrong about this.' He paused a moment, levelling his gaze on her. 'Why do you think I was going back to Athens four years ago?'

She stared. What had *that* to do with anything? He answered her silent incomprehension.

'I was going to see my parents,' he told her conversationally. 'I was going to tell them,' he continued, his tone still casual, still unexceptional, his eyes still resting on her, 'that I'd just met the woman I was going to marry.'

The silence stretched between them. Outside on the street she could hear the dim roar of traffic. But all she could hear in the room was the thud of her heartbeat, the pounding of her pulsing blood in her head.

Her mouth was dry suddenly, as parched as a desert. 'I don't understand.'

'No,' he agreed, 'you don't.' He paused again, then spoke. Said the words that were within him. That had been within him for all these years. Never said. Never spoken. Until now.

'I fell in love with you, Sophie, four years ago. I fell in love with the girl with almond blossom in her hair. The girl whose smile made my heart catch. The girl who enchanted me, captivated me! The girl I desired more than any other woman I'd known—ever could know. I fell in love with you.'

The silence was absolute. Not even the beating of her heart was audible.

Perhaps my heart has stopped. Perhaps I've died. I must have died—this cannot be real, it can't be.

She seemed to sway minutely.

'That's why I stayed with you that night. Because I knew you were my heart's love—that you were going to be mine all my life. And I knew you loved me, Sophie. Knew it with the certainty of one who loves. Every look, every touch confirmed it!' His voice changed, and something in it made Sophie's heart constrict. 'Every kiss confirmed it, Sophie. Every caress. You took me to heaven that night, and though

I knew I should have resisted, should have waited until I had made you mine as my bride, I could not! It was impossible to do so! So I made you mine in love, *with* love, mine for ever and eternity! And then—'

She saw his eyes shadow, and it pierced her—pierced her to the core.

'And then you told me what I meant to you.' His voice had changed again. Emptied. Become a hollow place. 'I wasn't the man you loved. I was only the man you wanted to marry. Because then everything would be "wonderful"!' He mocked the girlish gush of her accent, a mockery that lacerated like a knife across her skin. '"Wonderful!"' he echoed. 'Because then Daddy's company would be safe, and you would be safe too—the cosseted princess, Daddy's darling, protected from the world, cocooned in your music, your studies, your artless, easy, effortless life! And you would have Daddy, and Daddy would have his company, and you would have me, too, and everything would be just "wonderful"…'

She was white—as white as a sheet. Her face stricken.

She could only whisper. Anything more was beyond her. 'It's true,' she said. 'Everything you said. It's what I was. Pampered and protected. Totally indulged. Looking for shining white knights and silly, selfish happy ever afters!'

She could bear nothing more. The weight of it was crushing her. The weight of knowing that Nikos had been offering her a gift so precious, the gift of his love that she had yearned for, prayed for, and then feared she had only dreamt it hopelessly. The weight was grinding her heart to ashes.

If I had waited—if I had trusted him—

'I ruined it all,' she whispered. Anguish at what she had done stabbed her. What she had lost and destroyed. Yet through the anguish another emotion pierced, like a brilliant diamond light. *He loved me! He loved me all along!* Loved me all along! The wondrous joy of the realisation scintillated in her consciousness like a precious jewel.

But he was speaking again, and each word fell like a blow, shattering her brief joy.

'When I realised what I meant to you—a financial rescue package—it made me cruel. Vicious. That's why I laid into you. Said what I did and left you.'

She bit her lip. The pain was fitting. 'I deserved it,' she said, her voice low with self-hatred. 'I deserved what you said to me—what you did!'

'Did you?' The same light, neutral tone was in his voice.

Her eyes flashed. '*Yes*! I was stupid and selfish and spoilt, and I thought that if only we were married you would sort everything out for my father and save him from ruin.'

His eyes were still resting on her, never flickering by a fraction. But there was something in their depths, something she could not recognise. Something powerful and veiled. 'And if you'd never found out that day about your father's financial problems, would you still have tried to persuade me to stay the night?'

She dropped her eyes. Swallowed. He wanted truth—he could have truth. Deserved truth.

'Yes,' she said in a low voice.

'Why, Sophie? *Why* would you have wanted me to stay the night?'

She threw back her head. 'This is pointless! It didn't happen that way, so what's the use of asking?'

'Just answer, Sophie.'

'What *for*?' she countered fiercely.

'Was it because you hoped that I would marry you?'

'Yes!'

He was stripping her soul bare and she could not stop him.

'And you wanted me to marry you because I was rich?'

Her lips pressed together.

Against her persistent silence he continued, inexorable. 'But why would my wealth attract you? Your father was already wealthy. So why did you want me to marry you?' His interrogation was remorseless, pitiless.

She would not answer. What use was the truth now, when her lack of faith in him, her lack of trust, had ruined her life?

'You didn't want to marry me for money—there was another reason, wasn't there? *Wasn't there*, Sophie? A reason I could see shining from your beautiful eyes every time I looked at you! A reason I could taste in the sweetness of your lips every time I kissed you! A reason that was in every touch, every caress, every trembling cry that came from you as I made you mine that night! A reason that my hurt and anger has blinded me to! But it was there all along! And it was there that night at Belledon, wasn't it? *Wasn't it*, Sophie?' He paused, his vehemence stilled.

But still she would not speak. Could not speak.

'You were in love with me,' he said.

The words hung on the air.

Then, slowly, very slowly, she whispered, her voice as faint as air, 'Yes.'

Hot, salty tears oozed in her eyes. She turned away blindly, seeking the handle of the door. Her vision blurred as she fumbled for the catch.

Nikos's arms closed around her.

'Sophie! Dear God, Sophie—don't go! Why are you trying to go? Trying to leave?'

His arms were folding her back against him, clasping her to him, close against him, so close…

He turned her around in his arms, the emotion in his eyes pouring over her.

'If I had known—if I had only known four years ago that you loved me!' His voice was choked. 'But I thought you only wanted me for my wealth, because your father's wealth was threatened! That you only wanted me to save him—!'

He broke off. She was gazing at him, her eyes anguished. 'But I *did* want you to save him! I *did*! What you threw at me was true! I can't excuse what I did!'

His eyes were still pouring into hers, full and lambent.

'But *I* can excuse it, Sophie.' He drew breath, and she felt his warm palms pressing on her shoulders, steadying her, supporting her, though she felt she must collapse. 'I can excuse it. You had only just found out that the father you adored was on the brink of ruin! And you thought that I was leaving you. That I didn't love you as you loved me.' His face twisted. 'I should have told you—told you what I felt about you! If I had only told you!'

He took a shuddering breath. But he had *never* told her, had let her fear that she meant nothing to him, and she had been desperate to discover if her fears were false.

'It was fear that made you do what you did,' he said sombrely. 'I could have assuaged those fears with a single word—and by doing so learned then what it has now taken me four long, bitter years to learn. I would have given the world to know it then! That you'd loved me all along.' There was pain in his voice, and accusation too—against himself. 'But instead I lashed out at you—and threw you to the waiting wolves. Oh God.' His voice wrung her heart. 'When I think of what you have endured these four years! You were so young when I knew you first! Your father kept you so protected from the world! Oh, it was part of your charm, part of your innocence, but it made you so vulnerable to the harsh realities of life!'

His voice changed, becoming stark. 'And now I have learnt just what you had to cope with, what you had to endure, the strength and fortitude and courage you had to find, the nightmare you have lived year after year, blow after blow, with everything taken from you—the support of your stricken father, your absolute devotion to him to be where you are now! Oh, Sophie, it twists like a knife in me!' His face was sombre, gaunt. 'You were protected and cosseted once, kept so by a doting father. But you're not that girl any longer—you've proved yourself beyond all endurance by your courage, your love, your devotion to your father!'

His voice changed again. 'And I hope I am not the man I was until so short a time ago. You've humbled me, Sophie, by what you have endured. I made assumptions about you that were as false as any lie.' He took a heavy, razoring breath. 'I wish with all my heart you had told me straight away, that night I dragged you into the taxi when you'd escaped from that louse Cosmo! But why should you have turned to me for help when I thought so ill of you?'

His hands tightened around her.

'But I thank God for that taxi-ride! Thank God that I tracked you down. Followed you to Belledon. Because now I know the truth about you! That you felt for me then, four long years ago, what I felt for you.' His voice caught at her. 'What I feel *now*, Sophie, my dearest one.' His expression softened. 'As you do too.'

He paused, and now his palms lifted from her shoulders and his fingers cupped her face again, sliding with gentle tenderness into the tendrils of her hair. He was so close to her, so close, and she felt faintness drumming in her, beating up into her tightening lungs.

'Love,' he told her.

His eyes were rich, full with emotion, and she felt the faintness beating more and yet more, so that she could scarcely breathe with it.

'Love always.' He gazed down into her eyes, his own ablaze with a fire that would never now be quenched. 'My love, my life—my Sophie. Always my Sophie, from this time on. As I am yours—for all time.'

His kiss was as tender as his gaze, the touch of his lips on hers adoring.

There was light—light everywhere. Lightness and bright-ness and the radiance of the sun pouring into her after long, bleak darkness.

How can this be? she thought, amazed and dazed and daz-zled and delirious. *How can this be?*

How could it be that Nikos was kissing her, embracing her, holding her so tenderly, so lovingly? It couldn't be true—surely it couldn't be true? Yet it was! It *was* true—it was real and true and not a dream—not a yearning—but real, real, real…

The tears were pouring down her face and he was kissing them away, kissing her and murmuring to her, with a wealth of tenderness, and then cradling her, soothing her, as she wept against him, wept away the long, bitter years that had divided them.

'Oh, Nikos—my own, own Nikos!' She pressed her face against his chest, weeping for all that she had lost and all that had been given to her again. Radiance filled her.

He swept her up, swept her away, carrying her as if she were no more than a feather, thistledown. He laid her down on the satin-covered bed and lay down beside her, cradling her all the time. Soothing her and hushing her, gentling her and quieting her.

And then softly, sweetly, tenderly and gently, passionately

and lovingly, he made love to her—the woman he loved, the girl he had always loved, his own, sweet Sophie, always his.

As he was hers. Now and for all the years to come.

EPILOGUE

THE music room at Belledon was hushed. At the piano Sophie sat, fingers poised over the keyboard, gathering her focus. Then, with a ripple of notes, she began to play. Chopin, lyrical and poignant, poured forth.

Sitting beside Edward Granton, freed now of his imprisoning wheelchair, Nikos watched the woman he loved play the music she loved. At his side he heard Sophie's father give a sigh of contentment.

'So like her mother,' he murmured, with a world of love in his low voice.

Nikos smiled. But his eyes remained on Sophie. Always on Sophie, his beloved wife. How blessed he was, he knew full well. To have lost her through his own lack of faith, and yet to have found her again. He would stand by her side for eternity now! Love her for all eternity.

As his gaze rested on her, Sophie caught his eyes, and her own filled with warmth and tenderness. Nikos—her own Nikos! Love swept through her, borne aloft by the swelling of the music at her fingertips. How much she loved him!

Happiness filled her—a happiness that was almost more than she could believe! Yet believe it she must—it was in every moment of the day. Every moment of the night. And it filled this house, too—Belledon, which Nikos had indeed restored, but for themselves to live in, just as in that fleeting longing for it to be their home which had fired within her as she'd wandered its desolate, abandoned rooms. They were desolate and abandoned no more. Restored, as their love had been restored, they now gloried in their beauty. Gracious and welcoming, lapped by breathtaking gardens, Belledon was a home once more.

And not just to them. For not only did Sophie's father live there now, with his health immeasurably improved in the three years since his daughter had won Nikos's love again, but Belledon was a home to many others who, like him, had suffered the grim debilitation of stroke. One whole wing had been transformed to become patient accommodation, and the extensive outhouses had been converted to treatment rooms and housing for medical staff—the whole enterprise funded by Kazandros Corp, for patients who could not otherwise have afforded the rehabilitation therapies on offer.

And one of them was music. Sophie had set up a series of weekly recitals, here in the beauty of the music room, played sometimes by herself, when she and Nikos were in residence, and sometimes by the orchestras and music students of the local secondary schools, for the benefit of patients and staff alike. Tonight, on this mild spring evening, it was her turn to give the performance, and as Chopin's preludes, etudes and nocturnes flowed through the candlelit dimness, she knew she had found her heart's content.

How much I have! My adored Nikos, my dear, dear father, and... Her eyes softened with infinite maternal love as she played. *And my precious, precious son...*

Taddeus Nikolai Stephanos Kazandros—known universally as Teddy—was now a lively eighteen-month-old toddler, and the apple of all eyes. Sophie's father vied with Nikos's parents as to who could spoil him the most, and even to Sophie and Nikos's more discerning eyes their firstborn was without fault or flaw. Her expression softened even more. Soon they would all have another baby to adore, and already she was sure that she could sense the first flutterings of new life within her.

Across the room, her eyes sought Nikos's again, meeting his in love and joy and mutual cherishing. And between them flowed a message as old as time itself. The eternal message of love fulfilled, that no power could defeat.

millsandboon.co.uk Community

Join Us!

The Community is the perfect place to meet and chat to kindred spirits who love books and reading as much as you do, but it's also the place to:

- Get the inside scoop from authors about their latest books
- Learn how to write a romance book with advice from our editors
- Help us to continue publishing the best in women's fiction
- Share your thoughts on the books we publish
- Befriend other users

Forums: Interact with each other as well as authors, editors and a whole host of other users worldwide.

Blogs: Every registered community member has their own blog to tell the world what they're up to and what's on their mind.

Book Challenge: We're aiming to read 5,000 books and have joined forces with The Reading Agency in our inaugural Book Challenge.

Profile Page: Showcase yourself and keep a record of your recent community activity.

Social Networking: We've added buttons at the end of every post to share via digg, Facebook, Google, Yahoo, technorati and de.licio.us.

www.millsandboon.co.uk

2 FREE BOOKS
AND A SURPRISE GIFT

We would like to take this opportunity to thank you for reading this Mills & Boon® book by offering you the chance to take TWO more specially selected books from the Modern™ series absolutely FREE! We're also making this offer to introduce you to the benefits of the Mills & Boon® Book Club™—

- **FREE home delivery**
- **FREE gifts and competitions**
- **FREE monthly Newsletter**
- **Exclusive Mills & Boon Book Club offers**
- **Books available before they're in the shops**

Accepting these FREE books and gift places you under no obligation to buy, you may cancel at any time, even after receiving your free books. Simply complete your details below and return the entire page to the address below. You don't even need a stamp!

YES Please send me 2 free Modern books and a surprise gift. I understand that unless you hear from me, I will receive 4 superb new books every month for just £3.19 each, postage and packing free. I am under no obligation to purchase any books and may cancel my subscription at any time. The free books and gift will be mine to keep in any case.

Ms/Mrs/Miss/Mr _____ Initials _____

Surname _____

Address _____

_____

_____ Postcode _____

E-mail _____

Send this whole page to: Mills & Boon Book Club, Free Book Offer, FREEPOST NAT 10298, Richmond, TW9 1BR